BLOOD

I opened my arms and the guard fell into them, his lips on mine before I could move. Although his obedience was in question, his aggression certainly made up for the lack. I pushed away from him. "Slowly, lover, you needn't be in such a hurry."

"Ah," he said, groaning, his hands grasping at my waist and pulling me to him, "but you taste so good I need more than one kiss."

I laughed softly. "Here? I think not, my good captain."

"No?"

"No. We bargained for kisses, and kisses are all you will get. But I promise you will not regret them."

And now I turned the aggressor. I kissed his mouth, hard and hurried, pulling at his lower lip with my teeth, grazing him for that first delicious taste of blood. He lifted me toward him and I wrapped my legs around his waist, still kissing him, nuzzling the skin of his cheeks, giving a low purr of delight. "Perhaps," I whispered huskily, "for such a strong and handsome soldier, I can give a little more than kisses."

I felt him throb up against me in response and as his hands traveled under my skirts and up to my thighs, I took advantage of his distraction and fastened my mouth on his neck.

How fortunate that he was so strong and so hungry for a woman. When I bit him, he didn't drop me, nor did he flinch or fight. Instead he leaned farther into me, holding me tightly, letting my teeth sink deep into his flesh. . . .

Books in the Vampire Legacy series by
Karen E. Taylor

BLOOD SECRETS
BITTER BLOOD
BLOOD TIES
BLOOD OF MY BLOOD
THE VAMPIRE VIVIENNE

Published by Pinnacle Books

THE VAMPIRE VIVIENNE

Karen E. Taylor

PINNACLE BOOKS
Kensington Publishing Corp.
http://www.pinnaclebooks.com

For Brian and Geoff—the best sons a mother could ever have.

PINNACLE BOOKS are published by

Kensington Publishing Corp.
850 Third Avenue
New York, NY 10022

First Printing: September 2001
10 9 8 7 6 5 4 3 2 1

Printed in the United States of America

Prologue

The shimmering figure in the mirror is little more than a girl. Sitting before the reflection, she brushes her lustrous blond hair and studies her pouting image. Finally, satisfied with the results, she rises from the vanity stool and, with a flirtatious shrug, drops the white satin robe from her shoulders. The girl's skin is almost as white as the clothes she sheds; perfect and unblemished, it glows in the flicker of many candles.

She runs long, delicate fingers over her breasts and thighs, giving a high-pitched, tingling laugh at the shivery sensations the touch brings. The mirror reveals her as young and succulent, a girl only beginning to wake to the mysteries of life, lips yet unkissed and a body still only dreaming of the passion that awaits her.

Deeper in the reflection lies a huddled mass of bedclothes, underneath which rests the young lover chosen for this special evening; chosen for his strength, the curl of his dark hair, and the blue of his eyes. It was the eyes that had decided her on this man; the way they watched her over a glass of wine, the way they burned into hers. It is time, she knows, long past time, and he will be the one.

The girl smiles at herself in the mirror one last time, knowing she should not, knowing there are reasons to shun her reflection. Mirrors, she has learned, should never be trusted. Still, she looks on herself and smiles.

But you must know, *mon ami,* the mirror lies, for the girl's reflection changes and a demon grins back at her. The lips curl and snarl, the teeth sharpen to fangs, the eyes glow with lust and hunger.

The mirror lies and the mirror will always lie; I know, for I am she in the mirror. My name is Vivienne Courbet and I am no girl.

Like countless others before him, my youthful lover is deceived by an innocence lost over three hundred years ago, yet still perfectly preserved in my face and body. And although he will not have the virginal conquest he expected, rest assured he will be more than compensated for the blood he gives to sustain my evil, unnatural, and wonderful life.

Part One

One

Paris: the House of the Swan, 1719

I was not always the demon in the mirror. Once I was human. Born in the usual manner, I grew, I played, I matured. Attending church with Maman, I prayed, crossing myself in the name of the Trinity, believing in that sweet salvation promised us by the priests. When Maman died, I stopped praying, stopped believing. And when I was old enough to be bartered and married, I rebelled, setting my feet on an irrevocable path, one that I would not now undo even if I could.

Such a familiar story was my life to that point that I need not tell it further than mentioning the rebellious girl, the unrelenting father, the late-night escape, and the long walk to the opportunities of the big city; in short, nothing that hadn't been done thousands of times before and since. In time I found my way to one of the few places a young lady of my ilk could exist without the interference of father or husband.

The House of the Swan beckoned to me, the name seeming a good omen. Had I not been called Mademoiselle Cygnette by my nurse from a young age? Here, then, I thought, was a place for me to stay. To be honest, I had almost reached the end of my endurance; any place willing to take me in would have done.

The proprietress met me at the door, saw to it that I was bathed, clothed, and fed, explaining to me that such kindness must be repaid with work. I agreed to work in her house for a place to sleep and meals, but after two weeks of backbreaking labor, I discovered there was another job here, one for which a girl was clothed in fine garments and had her meals served to her, a job in which such a girl was courted by rich and elegant gentlemen. Not entirely innocent as to the nature of Madame's business and aware enough to recognize the cunningness of her recruitment, I nevertheless knocked on her bedroom door one evening, looking for a way out of the kitchen.

"Entrez vous," she called and I dropped her a curtsy in the doorway. She smiled when she saw me and clapped her hands together as if in amusement or joy. "Why, if it isn't our newest little swan. Come in, my dear, and tell me how you are enjoying the work to which I put you."

"If you please, Madame, the work is fine. And I am very grateful for your allowing me to stay in your house, but some of the other girls have been talking and I wondered if I might . . ."

She threw her head back and laughed. "I wondered how long it would take such a precious princess to tire of manual labor. But do you know what you ask? Tell me, Vivienne." She rose from her chair and walked toward me, grasping my chin in her hand and turning my face up to her. "Are you a virgin?"

Now I was not, but she had no way to know that, nor was it in her best interests to prove that I was not. So I dropped my eyes and managed a blush and she clapped her hands together again. "Marvelous," she said, with a wry chuckle, "never say more than you need to, my dear, and always let that blush answer for you." She nodded her head and rang the bell at the door. "You'll do just fine, my little swan."

"Madame?" Chloe appeared at the door in answer to the bell.

"Take Vivienne to the empty room, Chloe, and set her up with some nice clothes." She looked at me intently, then nodded again. "Yes, I think that some of Marie's dresses will do, but none of the darker colors. White would be best." Cocking her head to one side, she thought. "Yes, white. And pink. Something youthful, with lots of frills and ribbons."

So before I became a creature of the night, I became a lady of the night. I should be ashamed to admit that the life suited me, but so it did, perfectly. The other women pampered me, dressing me as if I were a doll, brushing my hair and exclaiming over its natural curls. Madame was well pleased with me; she contrived to sell my virginity several times, until rumor of my existence became fact. Odd, how the fact really made little difference to the men; it was not virginity they craved, but rather the feel and look of innocence, the sweet blush of first love, something that I was able to provide them time after time. In this, they proved easy to please and so long as they were pleased, my position remained secure.

And life was good. Madame discovered that I

had a passable singing voice and added me to the roster of the girls who could entertain the guests in public as well as in private. With girlish pride I looked forward to performing in the tableaus and dramas, loving the applause and the adulation. It was during this period that I learned how to read and write and speak a smattering of other languages. I was well fed and elegantly clothed, warm and secure.

As the days and weeks turned into months and seasons, though, I grew restless.

"Chloe?"

"Hmmm?" She gripped a brush in her teeth while she was dressing my hair, combing it with her fingers and forming it into long spiraling curls.

"Where were you before you came here?"

She took the brush out of her mouth and held up a mirror for me to see the results of her work. "*Très bon,* Vivienne. But it is easy when one works with natural youth and beauty. As for where I was? What does it matter? I am here now."

I shrugged. "I am curious, that is all. It seems to me that I have seen nothing of the world. First I was at home and now I am here. And"—I got up from my chair, walked over to the window, and leaned my elbows on the sill, watching the people walking by—"it is good here and life is wonderful. But there must be something more, something wondrous. I know that the world is waiting for me and only me to come by and claim the prize."

"And what would that prize be?"

I laughed. "I have no idea, Chloe. Which makes it all the more wondrous, don't you agree?"

She gave a disgusted snort. "You have read entirely too many of Madame's books. Chivalry and romance? There will be no white knight riding in to save you from the ogre. The best you can hope for is to save a little money against the time you will not be young and beautiful. It is true that now you are much loved, and men praise you for the softness of your cheek and the whiteness of your breasts. But do you think this life lasts forever?"

I sighed. "It should, Chloe."

Two

Then, one evening, almost one year after I had arrived at the House of the Swan, the owners paid us a call. Madame herself came to get me so that I could be introduced. I could detect her nervousness and her fear from the minute she opened my door.

"Vivienne," she said, glancing around in the room to see, I presumed, if I was alone, "you have been summoned. Messieurs Leupold and Esteban have come and would like to meet you." She fussed with my hair and fluffed up the frills at the neckline of my dress; her hands trembled and her voice sounded tight and nervous.

"Madame?" Never before had I seen her this flustered over the arrival of two men. "Who are these men?"

"Oh, my dear, they own this house. I merely run it for them. And oh, they never send word that they are planning to visit. No, sometimes the door just opens up and they are there. Voilà!" She gave a little humorless laugh.

"But why do they wish to see me?"

"They have heard of you, Princess. The men

talk and the women talk and you are very much sought after. Apparently"—and she gave another little laugh—"you have acquired quite a reputation in a short time. But come, we have no time for small talk. They are waiting."

With that she rushed me down the hallway and practically pushed me into her private bedchamber. There, surrounded by the heavy brocade and velvet of Madame's accoutrements, in front of a roaring fire, stood two men, the likes of which I had never seen before.

They were not particularly tall, not particularly handsome. Dressed sedately, their hair was dark, their skin pale. One might have taken them for brothers, not so much because of their looks, but because of the similarity of their demeanor. They seemed to me more like men of religion than the sort who would traffic in this business. Nothing would ever distinguish them from any other man one might meet. Or so I thought, until they both turned away from the warmth of the flames and fastened their eyes on me. I took one tiny breath, overcome with terror and delight, amazed at the depth of those eyes and the worlds they promised me. In short, before a single word was spoken, I was lost.

"Go." That word was not directed at me. Madame murmured a quick acquiescence, the door opened, closed. And we three were alone.

"Your name is Vivienne, is that correct?" The older of the two spoke and smiled at me.

"*Oui*, Monsieur."

"I am Victor," he said with a small flourish and bow, "and my friend here is Maximillian. Or Max for short."

"Monsieur Victor, Monsieur Maximillian." I gave them both my best curtsy, the one I had been taught to use before royalty.

The gesture was not wasted on them. Victor threw his head back and laughed. His laughter should have put me at ease; instead I felt a cold sweat trickle down my back. "No, girl," he said, grown serious again, "we are not royalty, in any sense of the word. Just Victor and Max will do. What did that interfering old harpy tell you about us?"

"She said nothing, sirs, nothing that could be considered demeaning. But she seemed"—I hesitated a second, then continued—"frightened. Perhaps because you own the house and hold the power . . ."

At this the one I was to call Max shook his head. "Perhaps, but I doubt it, little one. She is frightened of us because she knows it is safer that way. Humans have such a good instinct for furthering their own lives. But you"—and he gave me what I supposed he thought was a kindly smile—"you aren't frightened."

I laughed, a high-pitched and ringing laugh men often called enchanting. "No, Max, I am not. I have been afraid of so few things in my life. My nurse always said as I was growing up that I had the temperament of a man. That I would come to no good end as a result. And, well, here I am." I laughed again. "So she is proven right. But still I am not frightened. Life is too short for fear or worry."

"Is it, Vivienne?"

Something in the way Max said those three

words made me shiver in anticipation, as if he knew a secret I did not.

I smiled at the both of them, wondering what exactly was expected of me. Was I to seduce them both? Together? Separately? A soft knock at the door brought me out of my speculations and I crossed the room to answer. Madame came in without a word and set down a tray containing tempting little morsels of food, fruit and cheese and bits of bread together with a fine vintage red wine and three of her best crystal glasses.

She patted my arm as she walked back out of the room. It seemed as if she was crossing herself, but that was silly. Madame was hardly a religious individual. I shrugged, closed the door after her, and, on impulse, reached over and drew the bolt shut. "There," I said, moving over to the tray and pouring wine, "that is much cozier. No interruptions."

We raised our glasses and drank a toast. "To long life," I proposed; Victor and Max exchanged a curious glance, then pressed me to sit down on the couch while they fed me and fussed over me. When half of the food was gone and all of the wine, they asked me to stand in front of them.

"Turn around," Victor ordered, motioning with his hand, his voice growing stern.

I did so and when I faced them again, their expressions had become more alive, more animated. I felt a flush of excitement, as warming as the fire.

"Take off your clothes."

I had heard that phrase hundreds of times since coming to the Swan, and obeyed it each and every time. At times I would undress slowly, playfully, drawing excitement from each little movement; other times I would be hurried and frantic. The outcome, of course, was always the same. Never had the action been fraught with peril or fear; it had always felt as natural as the sun setting and the moon rising. But to stand naked in the presence of these two men seemed somehow an irrevocable step, final and forever. And I had lied to Max, for I was frightened, more than I had ever been in my meager years, more because I did not know why.

I wanted to run and I wanted to stay. I wanted these men to leave and never return, while at the same time I knew I would regret that parting for all of my life. Poised on the brink of the unknown, I froze, unable to move, unable to speak. Caught in the gaze of their eyes, I could barely breathe. The room grew unbearably hot, the flicker of the candles distorted my vision so that it seemed that Max and Victor hovered over me like two large and merciless birds of prey. I took one step backward and crumpled to the floor.

When I awoke, I was lying on the couch, my dress had been loosened, and the room felt lighter. Holding a glass of wine to my lips, Max knelt next to me. I smiled at him, rather shyly. "I am sorry," I said, "I'm not sure what happened. It was very strange, it seemed that the two of you were . . ." I couldn't finish the thought. Instead I craned my head up and looked around the room. Victor was gone.

"He left," Max said, easily reading my thoughts. "I asked him to. I suspect that the two of us were a bit much for you. We are not your typical gentlemen."

I laughed at that and reached over to caress his face. He jumped slightly at the touch, but then leaned into my hand. His skin was smooth, cool to the touch, and although his eyes reflected the flames of the fire, they were also cold. So deep and fathomless and yet, so dead. I lifted my other hand and cradled his face, mesmerized by his eyes, wanting to do nothing but stare into them forever.

"What are you?" The whisper escaped my lips before I could think.

"Do you really want to know?"

"Oh, yes." I breathed as his mouth came down on mine. "Oh, yes, please."

Whatever I may have thought of Max afterward, that night he was, for me, the perfect being. He seemed at once an angel, a man, and a demon. He possessed me in ways even I had never known possible. Bringing me to the brink of ecstasy over and over again, he tested my limits, my strength, my passion. The feelings I felt were not love, not for either of us, but I was captivated, nonetheless. Watching the light from the fire sculpt the fine lines on his ageless face, I saw his canines grow and sharpen in his pleasure, felt them graze my skin as he kissed me. I knew his true nature then and reveled in the knowledge, welcomed his bite, wanted the opportunity to give everything I had.

Before he bent to drink fully at my neck, though, he stopped and pulled away from me. I gave a moan of disappointment and reached my arms up to bring him back to me.

"No." He stood up and towered over me where I lay, gasping for air. "Do not tempt me, Vivienne. I am very hungry, but I have dallied here too long and it is close to dawn. If you feed me now, I will take too much and you will surely die. I don't have the time to replenish you, nor do we have the time to prepare a place for you. And I would not force you into this decision so soon."

He began to put his clothes back on and silent tears flowed down my cheeks. My entire body felt emptied, as if he had drained me of the will to live. I heard myself saying, over and over, "Come back to me. Oh, please, come back to me."

He laughed as he headed for the door. "Enjoy the dawn, Vivienne, for if I return for you tomorrow evening, it will be your last."

He did return. He drained me to the point of death, brought me back to life with his own blood, wrapped me up in blankets, and carried me away to my new existence.

I was nineteen years old; I would never age, never have to sicken and die. The entire world stretched out at my feet and worshiped me; life was an adoring servant willing to give me everything I could ask. Made forever beautiful and forever young, I never once regretted that evening.

Three

Toledo: the House of Esteban, 1768

"I do not care whether it's Christmas Eve or not, Max. I'm hungry, I'm bored, and I'm going down to the village." Even knowing that I sounded like a petulant child didn't stop me from voicing my complaints. "This place is as quiet as a tomb and it's driving me mad."

For the first fifty years, Max and I had traveled extensively, sometimes just the two of us and sometimes with Victor. That life had been nomadic and exciting. There had always been new experiences, new people, and exotic foreign cities to explore. But when a year ago Max had decided to acquire and live in his ancestral home, the thrill faded. I felt trapped in this huge drafty house, I was always cold and always bored.

"Vivienne, we've been through this a hundred times. You are too noticeable, too memorable. Must I remind you that the last time you went into the village unattended, three bachelors presented themselves the next day to ask my permission to court you? You make entirely too much of an impression on the local boys. They've never seen your like before."

I gave a dry laugh. "They have barely seen my like now. I can't have spent more than ten hours out of this house since we came here. I'm weary, Max, and so filled up with ennui I could scream. And let's be honest, I am not your daughter, nor your wife that you can order me about or keep me prisoner here."

"You are not a prisoner, Vivienne, but I worry about you—"

I cleared my throat, interrupting him. "Must *I* remind *you,*" I said, echoing his tone and words, "that I am seventy years old and more than capable of survival all on my own? I have already learned everything you were willing to teach me, years ago. Let me out, Max. Or let me go."

"And where exactly would you go?"

"Back to Paris." I sighed. "And haven't we had this conversation before?"

He laughed. "Yes, so many times that I can't number them." Then he shrugged. "Fine, go into the village. Find yourself a nice young man to feed on. But try not to be seen by any others. They ask questions, they are capable of drawing the obvious conclusions. This is my family home; I do not wish to be driven out of it."

"I understand." I jumped out of my chair and got my cloak. "Thank you, *mon cher.* I know that you are concerned for me and that you do your best to keep me out of trouble. But what you do not understand is that I thrive on that same trouble you try to avoid. You are happy here, hidden away, with your library and your cellar full of mice and wine. I need excitement and singing and dancing. And every so often"—I kissed him on the cheek—"just a little bit of trouble."

I heard him laugh as I headed for the door. "Vivienne?"

"Yes?"

"Be careful. And have Frederick ready the coach for you and drive you into the village. That way you can stay until the crack of dawn and still make it back here safely."

Christmas Eve and I was free at last. It didn't matter that Frederick would be staying quite close to me or that he was likely to take back a full report to Max on our return. I wouldn't expect anything else of him—he was Max's servant after all. I could ask him to leave, I could get angry with him, but it would do no good. He could not help obeying his orders and had been told, no doubt, to keep a tight rein on me.

So I ignored him as best I could and walked to the church. Services were just starting and I knew that I would find Diego there. Sliding into one of the pews in the back, I searched out the crowd until I saw him, seated toward the front, with his mother and father and an entire pew full of his brothers and sisters. Señor Perez was the second richest man in the village and Diego was his first-born. Young, handsome, and strong, his blood had the sweetest taste, honey tinged with cinnamon and cloves.

He felt my stare, turned in his seat, giving me a nod and a slow, lazy smile. My heart beat just a little faster with that smile; my gums tingled with anticipation. "Happy Christmas, indeed," I whispered as I slid back out of the pew and quietly exited the church. Diego would know where to find me.

Back in the far corner of the churchyard was a cemetery, lined with huge old trees. I walked through the graves for a while, pausing to read some of the names and dates. Most of them had lived fewer years than I now possessed and that fact made me sad. And pleased me all at the same time. If life was good and something in which to rejoice, why shouldn't I be pleased with my seemingly endless years? I laughed softly and spread my arms, curtsying to the assembled dead. "Pardon, Messieurs et Mesdames, that laugh was not at your expense."

I heard the service ending and knew that Diego would arrive soon. "Where shall I hide?" I asked of the closest gravestone. "Behind a tree? No, that is too simple. How about up a tree?" I inclined my head as if I could hear the answer from the grave and laughed again. "Yes, that will do. Thank you for the suggestion."

I climbed the nearest tree and sat on one of the lower branches, my legs swinging back and forth, waiting for Diego.

"Vivienne?"

I kept quiet and watched him move through the paths. Finally he stood almost directly underneath where I sat. I waited until he turned his back to me, then dropped down silently and came up behind him, putting my hands over his eyes.

"Surprise, *mon chou.* And a *joyeux Noel.*"

He picked me up and swung me around. "Where have you been? I have been walking here almost every night looking for you. Why can't I call at the house for you? Not being able to see you is driving me crazy."

I made a face, probably lost on him in the darkness. "It is Max again. He thinks because he likes to live as a hermit that I should too."

Diego shook his head. "He keeps you as a prisoner in that horrible place, not even letting you out on market days."

"That does not matter. Max has his reasons and there is no arguing with him. Let's not waste our time by talking about it."

Diego kissed me then, his lips soft against mine, his tongue darting into my mouth. Oh, but he was sweet. And when I was with him, I felt young again, although I was older than his grandmother. I wrapped my arms around his neck and returned his kiss, pressing myself up against his warm muscled body.

He pulled me down to the ground, still kissing me. Then pushed away abruptly. "I almost forgot, I have a present for you."

I smiled, deep enough to bring out my dimples. "A present? For me?" I clapped my hands together. "I love presents."

He laughed indulgently. "I know you do, Vivienne. And so I bought you this."

He handed me a small parcel, wrapped in a silk handkerchief and tied with a ribbon. I unfolded the cloth and saw a tiny but ornate silver cross with a delicate chain. "Oh, it's lovely, Diego. Thank you."

I unfastened my cloak, letting it fall to the ground, and handed the necklace back to him. "Here, put it on me," I said, turning around and holding up my hair. He fastened the clasp and I turned back to him. The cross nestled in the notch of my neck and I put my hand up to it.

"Thank you," I said again, "I will treasure it forever."

He smiled and kissed the tip of my nose. "I am glad you like it. Alejandro said that you wouldn't. He said that you couldn't possibly wear it."

"Why would he say that?"

Diego looked away. "He says that since I only meet you at night and since I come back from seeing you pale and tired, that you must be one of the walking dead. But no, that is nothing but nonsense. And what does it matter what Alejandro thinks?"

I laughed, perhaps a bit higher pitched than normal. "Yes, it is nonsense. But you must tell him that I meet you at night because that is the only time I can get away from Max. And"—I gave him a wicked smile—"you are pale and tired for the best of reasons. Because you have been making love to me for most of the night."

"I can't tell him that."

"No?"

"No, I would not tarnish your reputation. I love you, Vivienne. I wish to marry you. And tomorrow, regardless of what Max thinks, I will call and ask for your hand."

"No, you mustn't. Promise me you won't, Diego."

"But I don't see what the problem is. . . ."

"No," I said, perfectly serious now and feeling all of my seventy years. "You do not see. Nor do I wish you to see." I gripped his shirtfront and pulled him close to me so that he could see into my eyes. "You must not ask to marry me. I cannot marry you, cannot marry anyone. Do not speak of it again."

He moved back from me and I felt the fabric of his shirt tear under my fingers. "Vivienne? What is wrong? You do not sound like yourself. Why can't you marry?"

I sighed. "I am sorry, Diego, I just can't. And that is all I can say. Please do not ask me again."

"But—"

I put my hand to his mouth. "Hush, *mon chou*, not another word. Don't you want to know what present I brought for you?"

He kissed my hand. "You didn't need to buy me a present."

I laughed, happy to see that he had dropped the subject of marriage. "I did not buy your present. I brought it with me, and hid it. Somewhere underneath all these clothes."

He put his hands on me and began to explore. "I don't see any presents," he said, unfastening the ties on my blouse. "I will have to keep looking."

"Please." I breathed the word, loving the feel of his hands, needing his warmth and his weight. "Oh, please. Find it quickly, Diego."

And he did. We made love there in the cemetery for hours, testing each other's endurance and strength. And when it was all over, I nipped at his neck and drank just a little, not to feed, but to hold the taste of him in reserve, to savor as I lay in my lonely box in Max's cold house.

Four

Toledo: the House of Esteban, 1769

"There must be a way."

Diego and I had managed to meet almost every week since Christmas. Max had given up on trying to keep me at the house; perhaps he feared I might really return to Paris, leaving him alone. Why he feared this, I had no idea. It was not as if I provided him comfort or companionship; quite the contrary, we had begun to have bitter fights, when we spoke at all. It was much like being tied to an unloved marriage partner, without even the dubious comfort of the phrase " 'Til death do you part."

As a result, Diego became the one joy in my life. I, who had always lived for pleasure, who had always looked forward to the setting of the sun with relish and anticipation, was reduced to relying on a human man.

"There must be a way," he said again, "a way we can stay together always without Max interfering."

I gave him a long, discerning look. He had

grown accustomed to my strange life, accepting that I could only be with him at night, welcoming the taking of his blood that occurred every time we made love. There was a way, I knew. If I were to transform him into a vampire, Max would have to accept him into the house. There would be no danger of exposure to the outside world; Diego would no longer be a stranger to be feared and guarded against; instead he would become a trusted member of the family.

"There is a way, Diego, *mon cher.* It will be difficult, but well worth it. And we can stay together forever."

He kissed me. "I would walk any path to be with you, I would face the devil himself for you, I would die for you."

Such noble and endearing words, they were exactly what I had wanted to hear, making me ignore the voices that urged me to hold back, wait. I would not wait.

Seventy years of living had not necessarily made me wise; rather I was as foolish and headstrong as I had been at eighteen, always making impetuous decisions when I should have stood back and considered my actions. And I knew this about me, even at that time, so I had no excuse for what I did.

At first, it seemed that everything would be fine. Max was not particularly pleased when I presented him with his newborn vampire son, but grew quickly accustomed to the situation. After all, here was somebody new for him to intimidate and frighten and teach in all things vampiric.

And Diego changed in more than physical ways. He looked to Max now for direction and guidance, readily embracing the bloodthirstier aspects of his new life. I forgave him this little betrayal; Max was undoubtedly the better teacher of the two of us, and I still had Diego to myself in the long daytime hours when he slept with me in my coffin.

When he advanced to the stage of being able to hunt alone, Diego changed completely. Demanding his own coffin, he grew withdrawn and surly, never speaking to me, and rarely to Max. Every so often a body of one of the villagers would be found, dead and drained, brutally savaged. Since there were wolves in the forests and it was a particularly bad winter, the blame was laid there. At first.

Max reassured me. "The boy is young and it is all new and exciting to him. He's playing right now with his powers; he will settle down, no doubt, and begin to exercise discretion about his feedings." Then he ruffled my hair. "We are not all as civilized as you, my dear. You seemed born to the life, knowing instinctually those things you must do to survive. Even when they seem the wrong things. I did well in choosing you."

I laughed. "It was not much of a choice, Max. One night we met and the next, voilà! And I certainly don't know why you did it."

He gave me a sharp look. "Do you not indeed? Why did you change Diego?"

I sighed. "I wanted a companion, someone with whom to share the life. You and I were not exactly amiable at that time and I was lonely. It did not turn out the way I had hoped."

"No." He favored me with one of his twisted smiles. "It rarely does. But your reasons are close enough to mine. And perhaps your choice was just as good. He has certainly taken to the hunt quite well."

"Too well. I miss the man he used to be."

"Sometimes, the change is subtle, as in your case. And for others it is a life-defining event and the person they were before dies."

"What were you like, Max, before the change?"

He said nothing and looked away, but not quickly enough for me to miss the beginning of tears. Max? Crying? Anathema. I did not question him further, suspecting that I really did not want to know what tragedies lay buried in his heart next to the man he once was.

But despite Max's reassurances, Diego did not settle down. With each sunset he grew wilder and more violent; the dead bodies appeared more frequently now, most with their throats ripped out, and ugly rumors began to circulate through the village. Rosa, one of our new servants, brought in and carefully subdued by Max to act as my maid, would bring the gossip back with her and tell me, as she brushed my hair and dressed me.

"There is talk," she said, "of bringing the white horse to the cemetery."

"The white horse?"

"To detect the grave of a vampire. How could you not know?"

I shook my head. "But there are no vampires in the cemetery."

"Popular superstition has it that those who die by the bite of the vampire come back to life as one."

I threw my head back and laughed. "That is one of the silliest things I have ever heard. If that were true, then the whole world would be vampires."

She gave me a smile and then sobered instantly. "True, Miss Vivienne, but that doesn't stop the villagers from talking. They say that they will kill the monster."

I sighed. *Ah, Diego,* I thought, *my sweet-faced friend, I have done a terrible thing. And now I shall have to correct my mistake.*

"Diego?" I touched his sleeve as I passed him in the hallway. "Come and speak with me for a while."

For once, he didn't shake off my hand and he smiled, his eyes almost the eyes I knew. "That would be nice, Vivienne, I have not spent much time with you lately."

We sat on one of the sofas in the music room. "You must stop killing, Diego. Death is not necessary, you know this. Even you do not need to take that much blood to survive."

"Why do you assume that I am to blame for the deaths?" His voice was soft and sincere. "They could just as easily be his." He nodded toward the piano. "He was, after all, my teacher in all things."

"Max is not a killer," I said with certainty.

"No? Can you be sure? So sure that you would think it of me and not him? You know me well. Just how much do you know of Max?"

"Max is not a killer, Diego." My voice lost a little of its conviction. "I would have known before now."

"Would you truly? If he hid it from you?"

"Yes, I think I would still know."

"But you are not sure, Vivienne. I know this by the look in your eyes. Max is a dangerous monster, much more powerful than we could ever imagine. And who knows the sorts of games he plans?"

"Nonsense," I said, but he changed the subject, taking my hand and kissing it slowly.

"I have been neglecting you, my love, but now that I have learned all I can learn to make you proud of me, to prove that I am worthy, perhaps we can we share the night again?"

He sounded so like the Diego I knew. "It is good to have you back, *mon chou.*" I took him by the hand and led him to my room. By the time the dawn was near, I was sure that I was wrong about him. And almost as sure that I was wrong about Max. It was unthinkable that this lovely creature who rested at my side could be a killer.

"Still," Diego said, returning to the subject when we were sated with the touch and taste of each other, "I fear Max. As you should."

"We could go away, Diego. To Paris." I smiled and ran my nails down his perfect skin. "You will like Paris, I promise."

"Yes," he agreed, giving me a kiss and getting up from the bed, "we will go to Paris together, you and I. And then you will see that it is not I doing the killing."

The next evening when I awoke I was alone in my coffin. Only the faint scent of him held the reminder that we had been together. But I smiled as Rosa dressed me, thinking of the plans we had made. Paris. I held the name in my mind like a prayer.

Rosa seemed happy, she even hummed a little song as she brushed my hair. "Good news, Rosa?" I asked, thinking perhaps she had a lover in the village.

"Oh, yes, Miss Vivienne. The monster is dead."

"What monster?" I felt a small chill crawl up my spine and shivered.

"The one who was killing the villagers. So now there will be no need for the white horse, no need for a vampire hunt, and we can all live safely again."

"How did this happen? Do you know?"

"Master Esteban did the honorable thing."

"Max? Did he surrender to the villagers?" I could hardly believe what she was telling me. "How do you know?"

She laughed and shook her head. "Master did not surrender to anyone. What a silly notion. He was the one who killed the monster."

"Diego?" I whispered the name, still feeling the touch of his breath on my skin. "Diego?"

She spat. "He does not deserve his Christian name; that man was the devil himself. One of his victims was my sister. May he burn in hell forever."

"Diego!" I jumped up from my chair and ran down the hallway to Max's room. "What have you done to him, Max?"

"Vivienne, it is over. He challenged me and I won. I will have the remains taken down to the villagers with our apologies for harboring the monster."

"You killed him."

"An understatement, my dear, but yes, I did. He left me no choice."

"Where is he? May I see him?"

"I would not advise it, but if you wish." He pointed to a second coffin in the room that I hadn't noticed before.

I opened the lid. And screamed.

Diego's head rested on top of his chest. The wound was ragged. Max had torn him apart, it seemed, with his bare hands.

"How did you do this?" I asked, not really wanting to know.

He gave a bitter laugh. "I had not actually known it was possible. But I remembered Victor describing the technique." He held his hands up, parallel with the floor and fingers fully tensed and extended. "You drive both hands through each side of the neck, like so"—and he brought his fingers together in a quick, violent motion. "And when they meet, you push them up."

I closed my eyes for a second and wished I hadn't, since I could easily visualize the action. Somewhere in the back of my mind, I heard a voice asking, "Did the head fly far?" It was my voice and Max laughed fully now.

"You are amazing, Vivienne. I present you with the decapitated head of your recent lover and convert and this is all you can ask? I have underestimated you, perhaps."

I ignored him. "Diego said that it was you doing the killings, that he was innocent."

"And you believed him?"

I looked at him and dropped the lid of the coffin down. The echo of the noise sounded hollow and cold. "I do not know what to believe, Max.

Except that I wish to be gone from here and from you. I am weary of all of this and do not wish to play your games. You will give me ownership of the House of the Swan, I will go back to Paris, and I do not care if I ever see you again."

Five

Paris: the House of the Swan, 1792

Monique showed up on my doorstep one rainy spring evening over two hundred years ago, drenched, underfed, and disheveled. It was certain that she had no knowledge of whom she was asking succor. I doubt even that she knew what sort of establishment she had entered.

I had long since quit working and retired to the background, appearing very infrequently and always veiled, to disguise my youth as best I could. If any of the women employed at the Swan knew what I was, they kept my secret in exchange for the safe haven I offered them. The money they earned was theirs to keep, with only a pittance held out for expenses of the house. It was an equitable arrangement for all of us.

That night I was alone and sitting in my bedroom in front of a warming fire when Monique was brought to me for my approval. She curtsied to me from the doorway. "Mademoiselle," she said with a slight shiver in her voice, "I wish to thank you."

I nodded at the woman who had brought her. "Thank you, Rosa. Leave her here, but bring us some food." I took another look at the bedraggled creature shivering in my doorway. "And some brandy."

"Yes, Mademoiselle Courbet." Rosa hurried off. I sighed as she moved away. How had she grown so old? She'd been as young as I when first we met, and now she was stooped and crippled with age. Years ago I had offered her the chance at immortality, but she chose to remain as she was. I often wondered if she regretted the decision. Still, Max had always insisted that one needed at least one human servant to safeguard the long daytime sleep. And Rosa was mine, totally devoted to me.

Hearing a slight whimper from the doorway, I turned in my chair and beckoned to the girl. "Come in, child." I pitched my voice lower than normal, putting a slight quaver in it. I had learned the role of the aging Madame well by this time. Only the youth of my hands betrayed me, and those I hid with gloves. "And warm yourself by the fire."

As she walked past, I noticed that she moved slowly and gingerly as if in pain, detected a faint smell of blood permeating the air around her. I caught my breath. "Are you hurt, girl?"

She turned her face up to me, her cheeks flushed with the warmth of the fire, her eyes huge and haunted. "It will heal, Mademoiselle." She attempted a curtsy again, but instead gave a gasp of pain and crumpled up, dropping to the floor.

Until that moment, I had not realized that I still possessed human feelings. *In fact,* I thought with a dry laugh as I knelt over her, *I am not so sure I ever possessed them.* Perhaps something special in her brought out these emotions, perhaps I had merely gone too long without someone to love. Whatever the reasons, her arrival gave me a gift: the ability to care.

She moaned softly and her eyelids flickered.

"Poor little lamb," I whispered as I picked her up and carried her to my bed, settling her into the pillows as gently as a mother might, brushing a strand of black hair away from her pale face. "Let's get you clean and dry."

I stripped away her sodden clothing, shocked by the bruises revealed, marks of very recent violence. She had been beaten with a stick or some other blunt weapon, the blows seemingly concentrated on her abdomen. As I bent lower to wrap her in one of my own robes, I was assailed by a strong odor of stale blood and rot. Peeling away the putrid rags wadded between her legs, I found more, stuffed within her to stem the flow. But this was not her normal monthly occurrence, it was far worse and more serious.

Looking around the room to see that I was not observed, I dabbed my finger in the now freely flowing blood trickling down her thigh, held it up to my nose, then touched my tongue to it. The taste was bitter, tinged with poison and death. I shuddered, glancing down at her again, examining the bruises, the blood, the distension of her abdomen, understanding at last what had been done to this girl.

"*Mon Dieu.* And they would call me a monster." I shook my head, growing angrier with every second. "But this, this is truly monstrous."

The girl started to shiver and I wrapped her up tightly in the blankets. "Who did this to you?" I whispered to her, knowing she couldn't comprehend, much less answer me. "Who did this? Your father? Your lover? Who would be so inhuman as to beat the baby out of you and then leave you to die? Monstrous!"

I heard a step in the doorway and spun around to see Rosa in the doorway, a tray in her hands. "Rosa"—I gestured to her—"put the food down, but bring the brandy here. Then send someone to fetch the midwife and bring me some hot water to wash her. I fear this poor little waif may be dying on us."

Staring down at the pale figure, Rosa set the tray down on the bed table. She crossed herself and mumbled something under her breath. I gave her a push in the small of her back. "No time for prayers, woman. Now hurry!"

As she scurried out of the room, I poured a glass of brandy and sat next to the shivering girl, holding her up around the shoulders and coaxing her to drink. She sputtered a bit, but then drank, long-pulled and hard-swallowed sips until the glass was empty. I poured her another and she drained that as well, giving a drawn-out sigh as I laid her back on the pillows. Rosa reappeared with a basin of hot water, lavender scented, and a large assortment of washing and drying cloths. Between the two of us we had the girl cleaned and dried by the time the midwife arrived.

"One of your girls, Vivienne?" Marie slipped out of her wet cloak and walked toward the bed. She had long dealt with the House of the Swan and so her familiarity was permitted.

I shook my head. *"Mon Dieu, no!* I would not treat even an animal like this. She came in off the streets."

"Not a good place to be these days." She tossed the covers away from the girl and clicked her tongue. "Bad," she said, "but I have seen worse. With enough rest and care, she should survive." Marie spread the girl's legs open and gently examined her, shaking her head when she had finished. She dipped her reddened hands into the basin of lavender water. "The afterbirth, at least, is gone. I had feared from the odor that it hadn't passed, but fortunately I was wrong. And now that her blood is flowing steadily, well, that should cleanse her. What happened to the baby?"

I handed her a cloth to dry her hands and shrugged. "I do not know, Marie, she did not have it when she came. I would guess that whoever did this to her would have disposed of the child as well." I felt myself growing angrier than I had been in a very long time. *"Immonde!* And God forbid whoever did this should ever show his face around here; I will rip him to shreds."

Rosa shivered, but Marie gave a grim laugh and nodded. "Just so, Vivienne. I believe you would. Now, you must keep her warm and clean; after an hour or so, you can probably wad up some cloths between her legs to catch the blood. Your bed, of course, is ruined." She gave me a glance from the corner of her eyes. "Not, I suppose, that such a thing would bother you." I tensed, then relaxed when she finished her thought. "You have plenty of beds here."

I paid her and escorted her through the hallways and down the stairs to our back entrance. "Thank you, Marie, for coming so quickly."

She nodded and smiled. "You might want to assign someone else to watch her during the day tomorrow."

I had gotten so involved in the drama of the sick girl, I'd not even thought about arrangements. Of course I could not stand watch over her during the day or I would die, but Marie would not know that. "Yes." I nodded as if in consideration. "I can get Rosa to watch, so that I can attend to business."

"Or rest." She laid a warm hand on my cheek. "You look very pale, Vivienne. Be careful of yourself, my dear, these are becoming dangerous times. And I would hate to lose my most steady source of income."

She opened the door and I watched her walk out into the rainy streets, wondering at her warning. But she was right about these being dangerous times; I could scent the blood fury in the air.

Six

Closing and locking the door, as if to keep the trouble outside, I turned my veil down and moved into the entertainment room. Here the men would meet the girls and make their choices for the night. Since it was still early in the evening, the room was crowded and noisy, but fell quiet when I walked in, save for a whisper or two explaining who I was.

"Mademoiselle Courbet," one of the revelers called. "Perhaps you would sing us a song? The one about the earl and the milkmaid has always been one of my favorites."

I cleared my throat and smiled at him through my veil. "I fear, young man"—and I deliberately made my voice hoarse and harsh—"that I am past the singing of such a song. However, I thank you for asking. It is good to be remembered. Now, since you have been so kind and since I feel like celebrating this evening, good Messieurs, tonight the wine is free."

"How about the girls?" a man called out. "Are they free too?"

I looked over at him; he was quite young and

obviously a nobleman as well as extraordinarily drunk. I crooked my finger at him and he walked rather unsteadily across the floor to face me.

"What is your name, young man?"

"Michael Leroux, at your service, Madame."

"Ah. I shall keep your service in mind, Michael. But I must tell you that there is only one girl, as you say, here who is free. And I daresay you may not be man enough for her."

He looked around the room with a simpering grin on his dandy's face. "I am man enough for any woman in this room. Which of these ladies is to be mine tonight?"

I laughed and pulled him closer to me by the lace of his jabot, so close that I could smell the scent of bitter wine on his lips. "I fear, Monsieur, that you are slightly addled, perhaps by the grandeur of this company, perhaps by the fine wine we serve. No matter, for none of these women will be yours tonight. Rather"—I stared into his eyes through the veil, giving him the full force of my power and my smile—"*you* will be mine. Come."

I walked out of the room, never turning around to see if he followed. I knew that he would, he had no choice. As I started up the stairs, listening to his footsteps falling behind me, the room we'd just left became noisy once more with laughter and ribald jokes at Michael's expense. "Poor fellow," I could hear them say, "forced to make love to an old lady."

Pulling a key out of my pocket, I unlocked the door to the room I used for my assignations. Michael walked in behind me and hesitated at the door. "Sit down," I ordered and he settled in on one of the ornate brocade lounges as I closed and bolted the door.

I pulled off the veil that covered my face. "Look at me, Michael," I said.

"Perhaps it would be best, Mademoiselle, if I did not. I will just keep my eyes closed and—"

"Fool. Open your eyes, Michael, and you will have a surprise."

His fists clenched, but he turned and as his eyes fastened on me, he smiled. "You're not old, Mademoiselle Courbet," he said, blushing slightly. "I had always heard that you were old. But, no. You are young and beautiful. And I love you."

"Silly boy." I laughed, enjoying the obvious shiver this caused him and moved slowly toward him, unfastening the hooks on my bodice as I did so. "Beautiful, yes, and thank you, Monsieur. But I am old, older than you can imagine."

He shook his head when I finally stood before him. He put his hands out, touching my waist, then moved them up until he reached my breasts. "But your skin is so perfect, cool and smooth, like the marble of a sculpture." He touched me gently, almost reverently. And I sighed, loving the feel of his warmth against my cold flesh.

I leaned down and took his face into my hands, lightly kissing his lips, staring deep into his widening eyes. "And you, *mon cher gamin,* are so warm and so human. We could be the perfect match, you and I." He nodded and I smiled, letting him see my fangs. "Too bad you will not remember."

The skin on his neck punctured easily, his blood tasted rich and dark. He didn't fight. His hands at first still rested lightly on my breasts; then they moved around behind my head to hold my mouth to him. I pulled on him slowly, savoring each mouthful of his essence, imagining as I did so that I could see into his soul, that I could select and keep a piece of him.

I was hungrier than I'd thought, no doubt due to the earlier activities with the injured girl and the overwhelming scent of her blood. So when his grip loosened and his hands fell away from me, dropping limply to his sides, I knew that I had taken just a bit too much. My hunger was satisfied and I felt no need to drain him to his death; so with an effort of will, I pulled my mouth off of him and wiped my lower lip with the palm of my hand.

Michael's eyes were still open and his breath came in low gasps, but when I put my head to his chest, I could hear his heart was beating normally. He would live. But not to tell the tale.

"Michael." I knelt in front of him and grasped his face again, not gently, but purposefully. "Can you hear me?"

He nodded. "*Oui,* Mademoiselle. You have the mouth and the voice of an angel."

"Hardly an angel, *mon cher,* but I thank you for your sweetness and that portion of your life which now dwells with me. As a reward, you will find that you remember nothing of our evening. Do you understand?"

He twisted his brow as he looked up at me. "But I do remember—"

"No." Meeting his eyes firmly, I pitched my voice to be its most commanding. "You remember nothing. You came to my room with me and then you fell asleep. Too much wine, Michael, is not good for a young man with an amorous intent. You fell asleep and we did nothing."

"Nothing." He nodded, still dazed. "I had too much to drink and fell asleep. We did not—"

"No, we did not. In fact, you do not even remember my face. It is all a blur, as if washed away in the wine." I reached over and lightly brushed his eyelids so that they would close. "Sleep now."

I walked out of the room, refastening my bodice and leaving the door slightly open. One of the girls would find him at closing time and see that he found his way back to his friends. Or his friends would come seeking him out. It did not matter to me.

Rosa still held watch over the girl in my room. I sent her to sleep with the instructions that I would wake her before dawn so that I could take my daily rest. She nodded, knowing my ways, and smiled shyly at me. "She will live, won't she?"

"I will do my best, Rosa, to see that she does."

I changed into my dressing gown and sat for a while, sipping brandy and watching the flames of the fire. Michael's blood still warmed me, filling every inch of my body with life and vitality. By now certain aspects of my life had become boring. Most particularly I dreaded the daytime confinements, but the taking of blood was always exciting, always new. Such a lovely experience, leaving me full of energy and joy, enabling me to continue forever. And the varying tastes of the victims were so entrancing. I sipped again at my brandy and laughed. "Like the difference between fine wines," I said softly. "Michael, *mon gamin*, my, you were a young vintage, impertinent but sweet. *Merci.*"

My speaking disturbed the girl in the bed and she began to thrash around and moan. I took off my dressing gown and lay down next to her, covering us both with a heavy blanket. I whispered to her of sleep and peace and healing, glad that I had fed and was not tempted to weaken her further. Holding her like this, brushing back her hair and whispering, I was almost overwhelmed with affection and love. The question of why I should react to her in such a way did not cross my mind. I had never suspected the existence of one who could inspire such emotions in a creature such as I and did not bother to wonder why; instead I reveled in feelings as wondrous and delicious as the first taste of blood.

My acceptance of her was complete and eternal. She would be my daughter, my sister, my friend, and my love; anything else was unthinkable.

She rolled over to me and wrapped her arms around my neck, nestling close to my breasts. I could feel her warm breath tickling my skin. I smiled. Life was good.

"You will be fine, little lamb. I will take care of you, forever."

Seven

Monique recuperated quickly, surprising all of us with her strength and tenacity. After a week, she was out of bed, walking slowly but getting around. After two weeks, she managed to take over most of the duties Rosa would ordinarily do. It seemed a natural enough transition; Rosa was aging, after all, and would continue to age. Growing feeble as of late, she seemed to be withering before my eyes and I knew that I would need to replace her soon, regardless. So within a month of her arrival, Monique acted as my new personal maid and guard; she took my strange requests and requirements as if they were nothing out of the ordinary. I counted myself fortunate to find another like Rosa, suspecting Monique was so grateful to me for saving her life that she'd have served me even if I were the devil herself.

Of course she was more than a servant. She was my friend and confidant, perhaps even closer than that since she had been sleeping in my bed from that first night. We were not lovers, not exactly, but in her eyes, I'm not sure she knew the difference. After my first taste of her blood, she belonged to me. The experience of feeding held her in thrall; something I had done to make sure of her loyalty all the while thinking it was unnecessary in this case. She loved me as much as I loved her. I had made such an instant connection with her; how could it be different for her?

A timid knock on the door interrupted my thoughts. "Mademoiselle Courbet?"

"Damn it, Monique, have I not told you time and time again to call me Vivienne?"

"*Oui*, Mademoiselle. I shall try. But for now there are two things that require your attention. Rosa is very sick and a gentleman by the name of Maximillian Esteban is here to see you."

"Max? Here? Tonight? *Merde*. And Rosa? What is wrong with her?"

Monique shrugged. "I am not sure, Mademoiselle . . ."

I gave a small cough.

". . . Vivienne." She gave me one of her rare smiles, pleased, I thought, at being able to use my given name. "Rosa has been vomiting most of the day. Cook thinks that some of the meat has been tainted."

"Well, tell Cook to toss the meat out into the street and fetch the midwife for Rosa."

"And Monsieur Esteban?" She whispered the name as if it were a prayer, and a warning went off in my head.

I shot her a harsh look; her eyes were bright and her cheeks flushed. "You are to stay away from Monsieur Esteban, Monique. Do not disobey me in this. I will see to him myself."

She dropped a small curtsy and hurried back out the door. I sighed. *You cannot have it both ways,*

I thought. *Give her orders and she is a servant. And if she is not a servant, then you have no right to command her.*

"A new swan for the house, Vivienne?" Max's voice laughed from the hallway. "She's lovely. Nothing like a little new blood to liven up the place."

"Good evening, Max." I said, ignoring his laughter. "To what do I owe the honor of this visit?"

He crossed the room, picked me up, and kissed both of my cheeks before setting me down again. "Nothing special, Vivienne. Just wondering how my little French flower has been doing."

I glared at him. "She is doing fine although she has grown stronger thorns since last we met. I want no interference from you this time."

He sat down on the couch in front of the fire and stretched his hands out to the warmth. "Are you still angry?"

I gave a small puff of breath. "Do you even need to ask me that, Max?"

"No, I suppose I do not. But he was not right for you, you know that. He was too weak to control his actions and wouldn't have lasted more than a month on his own."

"But Diego was mine. And you hadn't the right."

Max nodded. "Yes, that is true. But you must see I was trying to protect you; you were younger then and weaker. An inferior transformation would have threatened your existence, our existence. He was rash and violent and would soon have brought trouble down on all of us. You did not know that at the time and I did not take the time to explain. I now give you my most heartfelt apologies. So do not stay angry with me and do not think badly of me. It will not happen again."

I stared at him for a while trying to read his expression and failing miserably. Finally I threw my hands up in the air and laughed. "I'd hardly think my thoughts mattered to you, dearest Max. However, that was a pretty enough apology and I see no need for us to be at war."

"Good." He patted the side of the couch; I walked over and sat next to him. He took my hand, kissed it softly, and then crooked it around his arm.

For a long time we sat together silently, watching the flames. He had fed recently—I could scent the blood on him—and as a result he was calmer than normal. For the first time since we met, I found his presence relaxing; had anyone walked in and seen us, we'd have appeared an old married couple, secure in each other and needing no talk, no touch. How wrong such appearances could be.

Then I felt him tense and shift in his seat. "And now, although I hate to bring up the subject, let us speak of the war here. I have heard of Monsieur Guillotine's new device, new at least to this city, and I wanted to remind you that beheading is one way to kill our kind. There seems to exist strange influence in this city; one that turns normal humans' minds to thoughts of blood and destruction. Be careful, Vivienne, that you do not incite the mob."

"Nonsense. What use would they have for my head? I am not royalty, not nobility. I am just a simple working girl. I do not get involved with politics."

"Even so, my dear, it might be best for you to leave this place until things settle down again. There is no logic to mob rule and that is where this city is headed. Let the others stand in the squares and howl for blood. You have no need to be involved. I remain safely ensconced in my ancestral home; you and whosoever you might chose to bring along would be welcome there."

I turned to him and smiled, laying a hand along his cheek. "You came all this way to warn me, *mon cher*? To offer me safe haven? I find that touching"—and I laughed, knowing that I should not—"but unnecessary, and we shall do just fine without your help."

His eyes grew cold and he brushed away my hand. "I should have known you would refuse my offer. But keep it in your mind, Vivienne. It may be that you are right, or you may still have need of a place to run to."

"I will remember."

He stood up. "I'll be here for the next month or so, my dear. And I will contact you before I go back to Spain in case you have changed your mind. Other than that, I will leave you alone. You have matured and grown well." He smiled down at me. "Even with the thorns." He began to move toward the door, but turned around halfway. "Do you hate me?"

"Hate you?" I thought for a second or two. "Except for the incident with Diego, I have no reason to hate you. You have given me eternal life and I am grateful." I studied the fire for a minute. "And you are right about Diego. I should have known that your instincts are better than mine; but do not tell Victor I said that or I swear I will tear out *your* throat."

He laughed, bowed, and turned to leave.

"Oh, Max!" Jumping up from the sofa, I ran to the door and called after him. "Next week we are having a masque; I'd be happy if you could attend. I assume you are staying in the old place. Shall I have someone bring you an invitation?"

"Yes." He nodded, then laughed. "Vivienne, I believe you would celebrate the birthday of Torquemada. What is the occasion for this fete?"

I smiled, feeling my dimples emerge. "It is true, Max, I do love a celebration. So this is my 'I am weary of this revolution' party, but do not give that away. No need to tempt the mob."

He bowed again and exited. I heard his footsteps in the hallway, the pause at the top of the stairs, the whispered "pardon, Monsieur."

"Ah, but you are lovely, my dear," he said, "so no pardon is needed. What is your name?"

My hearing was acute enough to catch the faint answer and recognize the voice. I felt every muscle in my body tense.

"And a lovely name, Monique." Max spoke again. "You are an intriguing young lady and I hope we shall meet at a later date. I would like to know more of you." She gave a short gasp and I heard him walk down the stairs.

"Not this one, Max," I said through clenched teeth.

"Mademoiselle?"

I spun around and looked at her. "Nothing, Monique."

"I could hardly avoid speaking to him, Vivienne, it would have been rude."

I nodded. To repeat my earlier warning might only make him more fascinating to her. So I shrugged and smiled.

"And how is Rosa? Did you get Marie?"

Monique shook her head. "She was out. Babies have notoriously bad timing. But I was fortunate enough to meet a doctor who heard me inquiring about Marie as he was passing by. He came with me and is seeing to Rosa now."

"Quite the fortunate encounter, Monique."

"Oui. And he is quite the gentleman, physician to royalty, he told me."

I laughed. "Every doctor in this city used to claim that title. But now? This doctor must be a foolish man."

Monique's eyes grew round. "Oh, no, Vivienne. He seems very wise and very concerned. I have never seen a man with such gentle hands." Her eyes darted away from mine and rested on the floor.

Poor little lamb, I thought, remembering not for the first time the bruises she'd sustained before coming to us, *I am quite sure you have never met a man with gentle hands.*

I nodded. "If you say so, Monique, it must be true."

"Oui, it is true. And he said he would like to speak with you."

Eight

I would not have been able to count the number of men I had met by this time in my life. There had been so many, in so many different capacities. None of them were able to resist me; with only one word, one look, they would come to me and feed my needs as lovers or as prey. Even considering the warmth of affection I felt for Monique, I had thought myself unmovable and untouchable in the area of l'amour.

Apparently, Eduard DeRouchard had been born to prove me wrong.

He was quite simply the most handsome man I had ever seen. A perfect example of humanity, he had a classic beauty: long golden hair, strong broad shoulders, and a porcelain complexion that would make other men seem feminine. For him, though, it was the perfect finish; stripped bare, he could be mistaken for a statue of Adonis. My first thought upon seeing him was that I must possess this man. And my second thought was that I never really could.

Eduard straightened up from where he stood over Rosa's bed and looked at me with deep green eyes. He then shook his head and turned back to her, laying a hand on her face, closing her eyes.

"I am sorry; I couldn't save her. The poison in her system was too strong."

"Poison?" Stunned, not just with the death of a valued servant, but with the presence of this man, I struggled to understand. "Who would poison Rosa?"

"You mistake my words; it needn't have been a deliberate attempt. Tainted food could easily cause the same ailment."

"Ah, I see. Nonetheless, I thank you, Doctor . . ."

"DeRouchard. Eduard DeRouchard." He gave an elegant bow, reached over to take my hand, and brought it to his lips. I felt myself blush.

"Vivienne Courbet." I stated my name, pulled my hand out of his grasp, and stifled the desire to curtsy. Beautiful though he was, and intimidating in that beauty, he was in my house and I was the mistress here. "*Merci,* Dr. DeRouchard, for your attempt. Poor Rosa. She was a good woman and I will miss her." I moved past him, laid a hand on her cheek, kissed her lightly on the forehead, and pulled the blanket up over her head.

Only then did I notice the great stench in the room; the odors of vomit, sweat, and blood permeated the air, a hideous assault on the senses that made me feel dizzy and sick.

"Perhaps, Doctor"—I motioned to the door—"you would like to clean up and partake of refreshments before you leave?"

"With a hostess of such great beauty offering such wonderful hospitality, I may never leave."

I laughed. "That, *mon cher,* can certainly be arranged."

Eduard followed me to my room under the watchful eyes of Monique. She trailed along behind us, hesitating as we entered the room, looking as if she were going to burst into tears or explode into anger. I smiled at her to forestall either outburst and gave her a kiss on the cheek.

"Monique, my lamb, be a dear and get the good doctor some food and wine. That's a good girl."

She glanced at me and then at Eduard.

He smiled at her. "Go on, girl, you should listen to your mistress." She dropped him a curtsy and left the room.

"I am not really her mistress, you know. I am also her friend."

"That is fortunate for the girl. You are, no doubt, less demanding because of that friendship. How long have you known her?"

I thought for a moment. "She came to us a little over a month ago."

"And now she is your maid?"

"I have been training her in that capacity, yes, since I did not think Rosa was as capable as she had been."

"And now Rosa is dead."

I sighed. "Yes. Poor woman. She had served me for so very many years."

He put his head back and laughed. "Cannot be all that much, Mademoiselle, for you can't have seen many more than twenty years."

"Very many years," I repeated, enjoying his look of disbelief. "And"—I glanced at him, smiling—"I am perhaps not so young as you think me."

I saw a glint of curiosity enter his eyes, saw questions beginning to form there in his mind. But a knock on the door distracted him and when Monique entered, the subject of age was forgotten.

"Food," she said sullenly and with less grace than usual, slamming down the tray filled with bread and fruit and cheese. Then she set a carafe heavily on the table next to the food. "And wine. As ordered."

"Thank you, Monique." Eduard got up from his seat on the lounge and walked over to her. "Are you happy here?"

"Why yes, Monsieur."

"And is this position preferable to your former one?"

She dropped her eyes. "I do not wish to speak of the past, Monsieur. You can rest assured that I am satisfied here."

"That is good. You must be sure to treat Mademoiselle Courbet with great care and courtesy and obey her. Do you understand?"

"*Oui,* Monsieur. I should know that without your saying so."

"Monique gives perfect satisfaction." I interrupted, wondering why Eduard should care for my domestic arrangements. "We were lucky to find her when we did."

"Good," Eduard said.

Monique looked over to me. "If that will be all, Mademoiselle Courbet, I think I shall retire now."

"By all means, Monique my lamb. Sleep well."

When she left the room, I turned to Eduard. "Dr. DeRouchard," I started.

"Eduard," he said with a smile. "You must call me Eduard."

I nodded. "Eduard, then, I fail to see why Monique's service should be of concern to you."

He shrugged. "It is not my concern, really, and I hope you forgive my impertinence. But she seemed rather sulky and I wanted to remind her of her duties. Girls like her often forget things in the heat of the moment. And that would not do."

I poured him a glass of wine and another for myself.

"Enough of the talk of servants, dead or otherwise," he said. "That is not the conversation one should have with a beautiful lady. He picked up one of the glasses and handed the other to me.

"And what shall we drink to?" I said. The touch of his hand over the glass was like lightning in the night sky and suddenly I felt unable to breathe.

"Let us drink," he said, his eyes staring into mine, "to the magic of the night."

And the night was magic. Or perhaps it was only Eduard. Not since Max had I met a man so capable of moving me.

And I was not thinking of Max.

From his first touch, I could only think of Eduard, with his firm hands and eyes that glowed with passion like torches at the palace. Seemingly insatiable, his body enfolded mine, enclosing me tightly in its heat. Never had I felt so warmed, never had just the touch of hand and mouth alone been enough to carry me past the brinks of passion, past the puny ecstasies I had known before. This was new. This was heaven and hell and all the good and bad things I had ever known—no, it was better than all of it. Better than feeding, better than blood, better than life.

And when he joined himself to me, I cried out

and my voice was savage and loud, echoing off the walls in the room, the houses in the street. An inhuman call, something wild, something frightening, it was the roar of the lioness within.

Eduard looked down at me lying naked beneath him, straining upward to pull more of him within me, holding him there, crying and convulsing around him. As I climaxed, I saw the buildup of his release tighten his body. The muscles in his arms tensed and glistened with sweat, his eyes shone like molten glass reflecting the candle flames. He shook and cried out, as loudly as I had, the lion satisfying the heated call of his mate. And then as he reached his climax and filled me with his seed, Eduard laughed. Long and low and full of pleasure and joy.

As he rolled from me, I gave a small giggle and a loud sigh. "Oh," I said and that was all.

"Yes," Eduard said. "I feel the same."

I ran lazy fingers down the side of his face, grazing him lightly with my nails, and he shivered. I kissed the trails that my fingers made and worked my way down to his neck, licking the skin gently, enjoying the taste of him. But my sensitive tongue felt a notch there, a hardened patch of skin. I opened my eyes and looked closely.

"But you have been hurt," I said, shocked at the ugly scar that traveled half of the entire width of his neck. "Eduard?" I said in amazement. "This cannot be what it appears to be. It looks as if someone had slit your throat, but then how would you be alive?"

He laughed. "Vivienne, my love, how can you doubt that I live? Have I not spent the entire evening showing you that I was, most certainly?"

I traced the mark with the tip of my fingernail and he shivered. "Of course you are alive, Eduard, and I am glad of that. But this scar . . ."

"I was a baby. My nurse was careless with a knife as she carved an apple by my cradle. It was not as deep a cut as would kill me. So rest assured, my dear, I am fully human and fully alive. And more than willing"—he pulled me into his arms again and deposited small tickling kisses on my face and neck—"oh, yes, more than willing and able to prove it."

I murmured something as he continued to kiss me, harder now, his mouth moving down to my breasts and my stomach, searching and tasting and taking me back to the heights of earlier passion. I curled my fingers into his hair and held his head to me and murmured something that may have been "love."

And so on that night, when death walked inside the house and bloody-handed revolution prowled the streets without, I made my second deadly mistake. Perhaps the first mistake of taking Monique in and nurturing her triggered this error. I had been warned, by both Max and Victor, that certain human emotions should be avoided. Pity, despair, and guilt undermined the instincts of a vampire; complacency fostered an unhealthy recklessness. I had at some time in the past fallen into these traps, but had managed to avoid the major pitfall. Even with Diego I had not fallen. I knew now that I could not have forgiven Max for his murder so readily if I had loved.

No, love, I had been told over and over, was

the worst of them all, for it demanded a surrender of self both physically and spiritually that was difficult enough for a human to manage. For a vampire to fall in love with a human meant death.

Death be damned, I thought as I lay in Eduard's arms, sated with our lovemaking, drunk on his presence, his scent, and the singing of his blood in his veins and in mine. "Death be damned," I whispered, fully willing to stay with this man until the rising of the sun.

Nine

Monique saved me from that fiery death by knocking on the door about an hour before dawn. "Mademoiselle Courbet?" she called from the hallway, "it's almost dawn."

Eduard rolled over and lazily kissed both of my nipples, then got up from the bed and began to dress. "I had not meant to stay so long, my dear, I will need to hurry away. It was a wonderful night, was it not?"

I smiled and sighed. "*Oui,* it was. Perhaps . . ." I bit back my reply. I did not need to beg a man to return. And although I did not understand the attraction Eduard held for me, I knew that it was an improper impulse. The best thing for me would be to show him the door and never see him again.

Fully dressed now, he leaned over the bed and kissed the tip of my nose. "I will call again, of course, dear Vivienne. And I can only hope that you will continue to receive me."

In response I shrugged and stretched. "We shall have to wait for that moment to see, Monsieur le Docteur."

Monique knocked again, her voice acquiring a note of panic. "Vivienne? Vivienne, did you hear me? Are you in there? Are you all right? Open the door, Mademoiselle, it is almost dawn."

Eduard opened the door and smiled at her. "Your mistress is quite safe, girl, I have not murdered her in her bed. Adieu."

Yawning, I rose from my bed and stretched again, enjoying the feel of my body and the play of muscles overused in the night of passion. Monique stared at me, shook her head, and began to prepare the room for my daily sleep. She fastened the shutters at the one lone and narrow window, pulled the three sets of heavy velvet drapes across. Watching her as I put on my silken nightgown, I could see that her shoulders were tense and trembling.

"What is it, Monique?"

"Nothing."

I walked over to her and set my hand on her shoulder. She jumped. "Nonsense. Do you think I cannot tell? You are upset about something, dear one. Tell me."

"It is nothing, Mademoiselle." She pushed the words out through clenched teeth, twisted away from me, and threw open the lid of my coffin, to shake out the cushions and sheets as she did every night. But her anger made her careless and the lid bounced against the bedposts and slammed back down, catching one of her fingers in the process.

Monique cried out and stood up, holding her finger before her eyes. Small drops of blood fell on the carpet, blending in with the dark red pattern. Tears welled up in her eyes and a low rumble of obscenities began deep in her throat like a growl. I could not catch the words, she spoke them so quietly, so hurriedly. At first I found her vehemence surprising, then shocking, and finally humorous. It was, after all, only a cut finger and she was using words not spoken in even impolite company.

She glared at me as I started to giggle, but I couldn't help my reaction. Her anger only made me laugh harder until finally she burst into tears.

"I want to go home," she wailed. "I hate you. You're cruel and terrible."

Home? I thought, getting my laughter under control. *I didn't know she had a home.* Then, I felt a rush of panic. *No, she mustn't go home. Rosa is dead and I need her.* Anxious to salvage the moment, I crossed the room and took her in my arms, comforting her as I remembered my nurse comforting me. "Ah, *ma belle petite*, it is only a cut finger. I will fix it for you."

Pulling back away from her, I took her hand and stared into her eyes, putting her finger to my mouth and licking away the blood. It was a small gash and had already stopped bleeding. "See?" I said, laying her hand on top of mine and patting it. "It is already healed."

She shook her head. "No, it is not healed."

"But . . ."

She backed away from me. "Don't you understand? It's not the cut or the finger or even your laughter. It is he."

"He? Eduard?"

"Yes. And you."

"I? And Eduard?" I shook my head. I could feel the approaching sunrise like a heavy weight in the center of my being; the dawn affected my ability to think and to function. I didn't need this argument, I needed to sleep. But I knew that I had to calm whatever fears and insecurities Monique had to ensure the safety of that sleep. "What about Eduard and me?"

She sighed. "If I needed any further convincing, this would do it. You must indeed be what you say you are, Vivienne. You certainly aren't human."

I gave a low laugh. "I have never led you to believe otherwise, *mon chou.* I may be a monster, but I am an honorable one. There have been no lies between us."

She thought about that for a moment. "No, you have been always truthful with me. And so that makes my anger harder to understand. You saved my life, you gave me friendship and companionship. I am bound to you, with gratitude and with blood. And yet . . ." She walked over to the bed and pulled the blankets and the sheets off, throwing them to the floor.

"And yet? So tell me, little lamb. How can I know what has hurt you and how can I make it better again, if you won't tell me?"

Her face crumpled up and once more tears flowed down her face. "You made love to him. In our bed." She kicked at the bed linens. "Pah. I can smell him in here even now. You locked me out and took pleasure with that man. In our bed."

I stood watching her for a minute as she gathered up the soiled linens and took fresh ones from the armoire. "You're jealous? That's what this is all about?"

Monique held the sheets up to her face, her

body jerking with little sobs. When she finally looked at me her face was blotchy, her eyes red. "I know that none of this means anything to you. I know I mean nothing to you." She gave a twisted smile. "I know that ultimately even he can mean nothing to you. You are incapable of feeling emotion. I know this." She stomped her foot and set the linens onto the bed, sitting herself beside them. "All you care about is a living body to warm you and protect you, a bellyful of blood, and a safe haven from the sun."

"But that is not true."

"No lies between us, Vivienne. Remember?"

I nodded and gave her a wan smile. "I never forget. And you are wrong, I do care for you, Monique. As if you were my sister or my daughter. But if you wish to go home, I will send you home, pay you well for the services you have given."

"Home?" She spat the word at me. "I have no other home than here. Not now, not from the night I came to your door and you brought me in under your roof. Do not taunt me, Mademoiselle Cygnette. The action is beneath you."

"Monique," I started but she glared at me.

"And how am I to be reassured that you do care for me?" She tossed her head. "How much do you care? As much as for Rosa? She served you faithfully for how many years, Vivienne? And seconds after she died and her body was still warm, you turned your back on her and dallied with a man you'd only just set eyes on. She deserved better notice from you. Did you give her a second thought? Would you give me a second thought?"

I sighed and sat down next to her on the

stripped bed. "I cannot help what I am, Monique. Nor do I want to. I am more than content with my life. That, however, does not mean that your well-being and happiness are unimportant. I understand I can't make you believe me."

"But you can. You can make me do anything you want; you have that power. And I have seen you use it, on everyone here but me. Am I so unworthy of your attentions? You should have left me on your doorstep to die."

I jumped from the bed and threw my hands up into the air. "You must be the most exasperating woman in this city. What on earth do you want from me, Monique? Tell me and I will try to oblige. Otherwise, I need my rest."

To my surprise she smiled, moved toward me, grasped my hands in hers, and kissed them. "I want to be like you. I want to live forever, to stay young and vibrant."

I laughed. "Is that all?"

"So you'll do it?"

I nodded. "At some point, yes, I'm sure of it. But not this morning, *ma chere,* and not until I can train someone to replace you. The both of us will need protection. And I would feel more secure once this horrible revolution is settled. But I promise I will do what you ask." I moved to the large wooden box at the foot of the bed. "May I sleep now?"

"Yes, sleep, my lovely mistress. And I will stand guard."

I climbed into the coffin, pulled the lid down, and settled in, waiting until I heard the sounds of her moving around the room to draw the bolts shut. No need to let her think I didn't trust her.

"But it is true, I do not trust you, Monique, not yet." I whispered the words as my body acknowledged the rising of the sun with a shiver and a sharp bite of pain.

But I did not fall asleep immediately, as was my wont. Instead, I replayed the previous evening over in my head, trying to remember each touch of his hand, each word from his mouth. I closed my eyes and felt the texture of his hair and skin on my fingers; I licked my lips and caught the wild, strange taste of him.

Eduard, I thought, *how strange you should come to me when you did. And how strange that I could love you.* Perhaps, though, the care and affection I felt for Monique carved a way for him into my heart. Had he come years ago, could I have made love with him, but not felt it for him?

"No." I whispered the word as I felt sleep overcome me. "I would have loved you at any time we met. I had no choice."

Ten

The next evening came and it seemed as if the argument between Monique and me had never happened. Even when Eduard called for me and we spent the rest of the night as we had the previous one, she was content and happy, even to the point of humming a little song as she brought him food. My promise that she would one day be transformed was apparently all that was needed to ensure continued peace.

As the days passed, though, I felt rather uncomfortable with that promise. I still remembered the look of Diego's body after Max had finished beheading him. I imagined Max's fingers piercing Monique's delicate neck, pushing their way through the soft flesh, and flicking off her head as if he were doing nothing more than plucking an apple from a tree.

I shivered at the thought and Eduard looked over at me, one eyebrow raised. He had been painting me, a skill I hadn't realized he had, and I had been standing naked for this pose, looking out the window. He set his brush down. "I am finished in any event. And you will take a chill standing there naked with the night air blowing over you."

I laughed and turned back to the window. "I was not shivering from the night air, Eduard."

"Then what?" He came to stand behind me and wrapped himself around me. I put my arm back and patted him on the cheek. "Shivering from nothing more terrible than having to stand still halfway across the room from you. But now you are here and I am warm."

He grasped my fingers. "No, you're not. You're cold," he said. "Cold as snow, cold as death. In fact, you are the coldest woman I have ever met, Vivienne." He laughed. "As well as the most passionate. A miraculous combination of fire and ice. Quite a fascinating subject."

"Subject?" I turned in his arms to smile at him and trailed a long fingernail down the muscles of his arm. "Is that what I am, your subject? Be careful, Dr. DeRouchard, those who have subjects are under close scrutiny. Monsieur Guillotine's device is growing more popular these days."

He sobered immediately and pushed away from me. "You should take this all more seriously, Vivienne. People, good people, are dying for less."

"I mean no harm, Eduard. And it is only you and I here now."

He laughed. "Yes, and we know each other so very well, do we not? I could be your worst enemy. You know nothing about me and yet you let me into your most intimate embrace. Monique had the right idea that first morning. I could have meant you harm. You are entirely too trusting, and . . ." He stopped and looked at me, giving me a huge grin. "Well, if it weren't so ridiculous

I would say that you are innocent. There is a war going on outside your very door, Vivienne. It may indeed pass you over like the angel of death. Or it may come looking for you."

I picked up my dressing gown from where I had dropped it on the floor when I posed, and put it on, walking across the room to the bottle of wine Monique had brought in earlier. "Why is everyone so determined these days to rule my thinking? First Max. Then Monique. And now you. I am capable of coming to my own conclusions and I am more than capable of living my life as I choose."

"Max?"

I poured two glasses of wine and offered him one. "Max is an old friend of mine. You will, perhaps, get a chance to meet him at the masque next week."

He made a noise of disgust. "And that's another thing. This fete of yours is ill timed. When there are children starving in the streets with no shoes to cover their feet, you should not be calling attention to your affluence. Won't you reconsider?"

"Tell me, Eduard, why should I reconsider? Because of vague fears? Veiled threats? It is not my fault the children are starving in the streets. Not my fault they have no shoes. I am nothing and no one. Why should anyone bother with me?"

"Because you call attention to yourself. You are affluent and obviously enjoy it. You are beautiful and flaunt it. And you are simple to think that you can avoid being remembered in the same thought as the aristocratic gentlemen who frequent the House of the Swan."

"Now I am simple? Eduard, take care you do not go too far and anger me."

"Come, my love, why should that anger you? You are simple; it is one of your best qualities." He laughed a bit, and came over to me, touching my arm.

I jerked away from him, spilling the wine I held all over the front of my gown. "Damn it, Eduard, look now what you've made me do."

It was silly for me to be angry, but that realization only made me worse. I was powerful, I was beautiful, and I would live forever. How dare he imply that I was stupid?

"How can you care for the state of your clothing and not care for what is happening right outside your door?"

"Eduard, my darling man, I know the danger of these times as well as you. And I choose to live my life in spite of them. So let us not fight over this."

"And if there are riots in the streets the evening of your party? What then? If innocents are killed, you can console yourself with the knowledge that you are living your life as you choose?"

I shook my head, bit my tongue, and held out the glass to him again. "Drink, Eduard. We need not fight."

"No, I should be going. And I think it might be best if I do not return. You are just a bit too careless of your fate and the fate of those who depend on you to make your company comfortable."

"Go then, you bastard!" I screamed at him and smashed the glass I had been offering against the hearth of the fireplace. "Run and hide like a rat on the street. But remember, being timid will not keep the mob away. Have a care to your own head."

He bowed to me. "You may regret those words someday, Vivienne. I can only pray that you manage to live that long."

I watched as he walked out the door. I regretted the words already.

"I think that's all of it, Vivienne." Monique had rushed into the room after hearing the sounds of the broken glass and my screaming. She got up from the floor where she had been picking up the shards and put them into the refuse basket.

I thanked her. "If I were being melodramatic, I would tell you that, should you find them, any remaining portions of my broken heart can be thrown into the fire."

Monique laughed. "But you would never be melodramatic. Nor"—she gave me a sly glance out of the corner of her eyes—"do you have a heart."

Giving a small chuckle, I wrapped my arms around myself. "No heart. You are right there. I keep giving it away to bastards."

"I saw his face as he went down the stairs, Vivienne. It must have been a good fight. Would it help if I said I was sorry?"

"No."

"Then . . ." She paused a bit. "It probably wouldn't be a good idea for me to say I warned you."

I flopped down onto the couch with a sigh.

"You can say it, you should say it. And then you should keep saying it until I listen. Love? What was I thinking?"

She came over behind me and rested her head on my shoulder. "You were thinking you were lonely and that you wanted to love and to be loved. No crime in that. And maybe you couldn't help yourself. Sometimes attraction is intense, and he has more than his share of magnetism."

"Just so." I sighed. "He is perfect, though. I should not have lost my temper."

"You are entitled to lose your temper, Vivienne. And he is not perfect, he just looks so."

"And acts perfect. And his hands are perfect and his mouth and the taste of him, his eyes, his voice, his soul. Everything about Eduard is perfect." I sighed and got up from the couch. I glanced at the painting he had been working on and wanted to cry. "Oh, Monique, I miss him already. He is my only and my perfect love."

A wicked smiled crossed her face. "No, Vivienne, he is not. But I have thought in what way he would meet your description. And decided that what he is, is the perfect bastard."

"Monique!"

"You know it is true, Mademoiselle. Eduard is a bastard, like all men. But being Eduard DeRouchard, he must do it much better than the normal man."

I shook my head and smiled. "It is true, Monique, he does do everything better than the normal man. Were he just a common bastard, I could not have given myself as I did."

She walked over to the dressing table, picked up my hair brush and walked back. "And that is your problem, Vivienne. You give yourself where you should not. I am surprised that you have lived as long as you have. On what?"

"Instincts, my lamb, I live on my instincts. And while I may have been fool enough to fall in love with the man, I never did trust him. At least not as much as you seem to think I did." It was a lie, of course. I trusted him completely and unreservedly, though I would not admit to the fact.

Instead, I leaned into her as she brushed my hair and let out a low purr of contentment. "Instincts," I said again, "are all I have."

"Then," Monique said dryly, "your instincts must be very good. Will you train me as well?"

I laughed. "Better, I hope."

"So when shall we start?"

I hesitated. "Let me speak with Max first."

"Max? Monsieur Esteban? What has he to do with it?"

"Everything and nothing, Monique. Please let it rest until then. One of the first things you must learn is to consider consequences."

"A lesson in which you, no doubt, excelled."

I slapped her gently on the arm. "Hush. You are getting entirely too sassy for a servant."

She took my hand, kissed it, and held it against her cheek. "We are more than servant and mistress. We are two halves of a whole, light and dark. Come to the mirror and I will show you."

She led me to the mirror and eased the dressing gown from my body. And then she stripped off her clothes and we both stood naked, side by side, staring at our reflections.

My skin glowed white in the flicker of the candles; her olive skin seemed to absorb the light. My hair shone yellow, like the sun I now shunned, and her head was as dark as a moonless sky. The bruises on her abdomen were faint now, barely visible, but I remembered how she had been mistreated before she had found her way to this house.

I reached over to gently stroke her stomach, feeling again the rush of anger I had felt on her arrival. "Do you still hurt, *ma chere?*"

She put her hand over top of mine and smiled. "I ache sometimes, but it is fine."

"I have asked you many times, Monique, who it was that beat you. And you have never answered. I can see that they suffer the same fate, if only you tell me."

She shrugged. "It doesn't matter. That was in the past and I am here now. And there are compensations."

"Compensations?"

"Oh, yes." She turned to me in the near darkness and touched my naked shoulder. "There are compensations. I have you now. And you are beautiful." She kissed the shoulder she'd touched. "And kind." She kissed my neck and ran her tongue up to my ear. "And passionate." She breathed the word into my ear and I laughed softly.

"That tickles, Monique."

"Shall I stop, Mademoiselle?"

She continued kissing my ear and her hand reached up and caressed my breast, teasing the nipple into erectness. "If you want me to stop," she said again, "you only need to say so. But I think you should let yourself go. And trust the one person who loves you the most."

I sighed. She was not Eduard, but her hands felt so good on my body, her breath was sweet and soft, and I gave myself over to her passions.

Eleven

Shortly before dawn, I crawled out of bed, away from Monique's entwining limbs and hair, and went to the window. The only light inside the room came from the now dying fire, so, still naked, I pulled the curtains aside, opened the shutters, and stared out into the narrow, dirty streets. Somewhere, not all that far away, stood the guillotine, both beloved and hated by the people of my country.

I wondered, and not for the first time, about this strange preoccupation the city seemed to have with death; how many lives had been taken by that cool and gleaming blade, how many of the necks sacrificed on that bloody altar had once been touched by my lips and teeth? I closed my eyes and stretched my own neck out, imagining the terror experienced. Once again I pondered the nature of human beings; they would consider me a monster for the life I led, for the small amount of blood I stole. And yet they inflicted far more horrible crimes on each other and called it justice.

I shook my head and gave a low laugh as I refastened the shutters and closed the draperies. Just as they would never understand my kind, I would never fathom them. "Fair enough," I whispered and walked over to the bed, staring for a while at the sleeping girl. Then I leaned over her, pulling the blankets up around her shoulders. "You may scoff, little lamb," I said quietly, "at my inability to care. And yet, you live only because I can and do love."

She rolled over and smiled in her sleep, whispering a name I couldn't hear. I longed to climb back into bed with her, to warm my cold body against hers, but the sun was rising and the coffin awaited.

I was not so foolish and headstrong as to completely ignore the wise warnings of both Max and Eduard about my planned masque. It was undoubtedly a bad time to celebrate anything at all. And yet, to my mind, that was one of the best reasons to proceed. Besides, I'd already had my costume made and the girls seemed to be looking forward to the change.

With a thought to the starving children Eduard had alluded to, as well as a hope to avoid giving offense to the mob, I gave orders to the kitchen staff that they prepare four times as much food as the number of party guests warranted. They were to hold the extra victuals in the kitchen and distribute to anyone who happened to call at the back door, whether begging or demanding.

"Even if they come back for more," I told Cook, "give them food until we run out. We do not need any trouble, especially not with so many people here that evening."

She nodded. I knew that some of the food would find its way into her baskets for distribution to her friends later on. It did not matter; the whole situation was a token appeasement at best. I hoped only that I would be considered a small target, hardly worth bothering when one had nobility and royalty to condemn and centuries of injustices for which to be recompensed.

To be honest, I had a difficult time understanding the conflict; there was plenty of everything to go around. Simple redistribution should not have to be so painful. So the sympathies I had rested with both sides. And with neither.

Now the guillotine, that was a different matter entirely. It seemed to me like so many human advancements—a total waste of energy and time and, in this case, blood.

Not that I was likely to knock on the palace doors and complain. I laughed to myself as the image of this crossed my mind. *Excuse me, Your Majesties,* and of course I would do my most practiced curtsy, keeping my eyes down in respect and humility, *did you know that gallons and gallons of blood are being wasted every day in the square? And did you know that this very blood could feed so many hungry vampires?*

And the king would be courteous and gallant. *Oh, my dear Mademoiselle Courbet,* he would say, *this is a travesty and an outrage. We would stop such cruelty if we could. But since we cannot, we shall at least send someone over to collect the waste, just for you.*

Perhaps I should attempt to take the castle in the dead of night and transform the both of them into monsters like myself. The queen would then refrain from exciting riot by her suggestions of the choice of solid food for the peasants. Or would she still persist in her innocent folly, saying, "Let them drink blood"?

I shook my head, laughing out loud as I opened the door to my room. I supposed that everyone was right; I did not take the current political situation seriously enough. But I was what I was and this very human battle meant nothing to me.

My room was dark and I noticed that the shutters were open; a light mist had curled in, filling the corners of the room, visible only by the faint light of the embers of the unbanked fire. "Monique should not have left these open," I said as I crossed the floor and closed the window against the night. "Anything or anyone could come in." Then I thought again of the queen and how those words I had given her would sound so delightful. I laughed at it once more.

"It must be a good jest, Vivienne. It does my lonely heart good to hear your laughter. And do not chide Monique for the open windows; that was my doing."

I jumped and turned. A lone figure was standing by the bed, elegantly dressed in a black velvet coat and breeches. "Victor!" I ran over to him and gave him a light kiss on each cheek. "But Max did not tell me you were here."

"Because, most likely, when Max called last, I was not here. I think"—and he lowered his voice somewhat, as if imparting a secret wisdom—"there are many of us gathered in this city now, more than you know, more than even I do. It is, perhaps, the scent of blood that draws us; like carrion crows we are called to scenes of war and death."

I twisted my mouth, trying to stop the giggle that threatened to escape. It was no good.

"Ever lighthearted, Vivienne?" He sounded offended. "I had hoped that the years would have begun to take their toll on your high spirits. But still you laugh."

"As often and as well as possible, Victor. It is usually the only answer that serves."

He shrugged. "Maybe you are right, my dear. But don't you worry about your welfare and safety?"

"*Sacre bleu!* Why is everyone so damnably concerned with my well-being all of a sudden? I have managed thus far and managed well. I am careful of those things that matter. As for the rest, it is nonsense. Why should I care why you have been drawn to the city? You are more than welcome to lap up the copious blood being spilt here."

"Even if that blood is yours?"

I narrowed my eyes and approached him. "Is that a threat, Victor? Yes, I have kept my sense of humor over the years, and I am truly sorry if that offends your vampiric sensibilities. However, I assure you that my instincts are just as finely honed as yours and I am as prepared to defend my existence as you are."

It was Victor's turn to laugh now. "Good. No, my dear, it was not a threat. Just a concern. I enjoy your presence too much to want to see your life end so soon. And certainly not by my hands or teeth." He walked over to the small serving table and pulled the top off of the carafe of wine. "May I?"

"Oh, certainly. Your unexpected arrival put all thoughts of hospitality out of my mind. Please, be my guest and help yourself."

He poured one for both of us and handed me a glass, clicking his up against mine and nodding. "And now, I must say something about that unfortunate occurrence that caused you and Max to part company."

"No. You must do nothing of the sort. I have spoken with Max about it."

"And you have forgiven him?"

"No."

"But surely after all this time—"

"No."

"I merely thought—"

"No! What Max did is unforgivable. That he did it with the best of intentions makes no difference. That he was right about Diego makes no difference. Diego was mine, to make or unmake."

"Ah." He drained his glass and poured another. "So it was not the act of killing that was reprehensible to you, but rather an issue of who was responsible?"

I shook my head. "It hardly matters, Victor. Diego is dead and that is that. I know better now than to trust Max." *And,* I thought, *you—since you have come here to plead his case.* "It's not as if I had any rights under law; I could hardly bring this before a human court."

"But what if we, as vampires, had a court? A group of us bound together with our shared needs and goals? We could prevent these sorts of unfortunate incidents from occurring, we could ensure the continuation of our species, eliminate the risk of human intervention in our affairs."

I laughed. "A cadre of vampires? And this is why you have come here at this time? To get support?"

He nodded. "As I have said, many of the others are here at the moment. Drawn to the turmoil and death. Or perhaps causing it. However, this seems like a perfect opportunity to find agreements and alliances. To govern those that need governing."

"But why involve me, Victor? I have no interest, no concerns that I can't handle myself. And I certainly have no great desire to govern. I have seen what happens to those who try to rule the world and it is not a pretty sight."

"But you will not oppose me?"

I gave a little shrug of my shoulders. "Provided you are not stepping on my toes, Victor, you may do what you like. I am, quite frankly, surprised that you would even take the time to ask; what possible difference could my support or lack thereof make? I am just a girl, getting by the best that I can."

He smiled. "You are more than you know, my dear, but we shall save that discussion for later. Except for me to say that I am pleased you have done so well. Most of our kind don't make it past the first fifty or so years. They get careless or suicidal."

"I can assure you, *mon gars,* that I am neither."

"Good." He poured himself another glass of my wine and drained it. "Now tell me about this little celebration you are planning."

I shrugged. "There is nothing to tell. It is a masquerade and it will be held tomorrow evening, regardless of the damned revolution, and"—I gave him a warning look—"regardless of what everyone thinks of it being ill-advised."

Victor stood up and shook his head. "I would not presume to advise you, my dear." He paused, but ignored my slight snicker. "I was merely hoping to gain an invitation."

"Done."

He bowed. "Then, until tomorrow evening, I bid you farewell."

Twelve

The night of the party arrived without any of the predictions of the doomsayers coming true. We were not mobbed and no one was dragged from the house to be set up on the guillotine platform. The first of the guests arrived while I was still dressing; no easy feat, this, since my costume was quite elaborate and Monique kept fussing over how the feathers would not lie properly, how my headdress would slide from one side to the other with my slightest motion.

"Enough," I said as she shifted the swan's head for the hundredth time, "we will just say that I am a drunken swan and leave it at that." Giving her a slight push, I held the white feathered mask up to my face and looked over my mirrored image. "Mademoiselle Cygnette," I said, curtsying and giggling. "If only my old nurse could see me now."

"Vivienne?"

"Ah, when I was young, I spent an extraordinary amount of time splashing in puddles and pools on my father's estate. That habit, plus the fact that I was very slim with a very long neck, is what earned me the nickname. It has nothing whatsoever to do with the name of this house. That, you see, was a pleasant coincidence."

She smiled. "For whatever reason the name was given, it certainly suits you."

"And you, my lamb? Are you going to get into costume soon? Or will you be spending the night watching the fete from the top of the stairs?"

"I only need a short time to prepare. You should go downstairs without me, though. I do not want to spoil your entrance."

I nodded and the swan's beak bobbed down in front of my eyes. I tugged at the back of the wig on which it rested to straighten it out. "I should have dressed as something simple, like a monk. This is much too top-heavy; I feel as if I might topple down the stairs if I move too quickly."

Monique gave me one of her rare laughs. "Imagine, you as a monk. Just don't make any sudden movements"—she adjusted the hat again—"and you should be fine."

I gave her a doubtful look and started to nod, but thought better of it. Instead I turned and slowly glided out of the door, my neck held high and stiff. I took the stairs carefully, holding up the costume's skirts and enormous train with one hand, gripping the banister with the other. A man dressed as a harlequin, replete in red and black and trimmed with golden bells, waited for me at the bottom of the stairs, holding out his arm to me as I approached.

Even with the number of people already in attendance, their human aromas mingling with the nauseating odors of food, I could discern his own unique scent. "Eduard." His name escaped my lips like a sigh, my heart jumped, and I felt breathless. I cleared my throat to disguise the fact that his appearance moved me as it did. *Damn this man,* I thought, *I should not react this way, like a young girl in the flush of first love. This is my world and I am mistress here. How can he affect me so?*

"My dear Vivienne," he said, his deep voice pitched so that only I could hear, "I tried, but I could not stay away. Do you forgive me?"

"Forgive you? For not being able to stay away?" Finally reaching the bottom of the stairs, I laughed and kissed him. "I am the one who should apologize; having ordered you out for nothing more than concern for me, knowing all the while that I would regret my actions."

"And did you?"

My mouth twisted up into a wry grin. "You know very well I did, Eduard. Half of Paris must have heard me screaming at you that evening."

He laughed, as I intended him to. "No, you silly goose, do you regret your actions?"

I turned my head slowly and gave him a long, cool look. "I suppose that depends entirely upon yours. And if you persist in calling me a goose, when any fool can see that I am a swan, I will throw you out again."

"But I am not just any fool, Vivienne. I am your fool."

"Are you, Eduard?" I looked at him closely, searching for signs of sarcasm and finding none. "Are you really?"

"Yes, of course. And now, Mademoiselle Cygnette, kindly do me the honor of granting me the next dance."

I should have expected that he would excel at

dancing as he did at everything else. Was there nothing he couldn't do and do well? *Damn the man,* I thought again, *why does he have to be so perfect?* He put his hand to my waist and I trembled, feeling I could dance with him forever, feeling that I could spread my artificial swan's wings and fly, deep into the night sky, far away from the hunger and the blood, to be nourished only by his touch and his smile.

Apparently Eduard was not the only fool present.

As we moved around the room, swaying and spinning to the music, I caught glimpses of people I knew; the gaudy colors and fabrics of their garb blended with their faces as we whirled past. The room grew strangely distorted, almost unreal, as if my emotions had become visible, generating waves of heat. Only Eduard and I existed; the rest was mirage.

Monique stood up against the wall, dressed as a shepherdess, all ribbons and bows and lace. She had her arms crossed, mask in one hand and crook in the other. I thought for a moment that she was glaring at me in hatred, but no, I must have been mistaken, for as we danced closer, her face lit up and she smiled at me, blowing me a kiss. Then she nodded to Eduard and moved off to another area of the room, joining in conversation with a monk and a grim reaper.

When the song ended, the dancers stopped in their places and applauded the musicians. Eduard leaned over and kissed my hand, his breath warming my skin. I blushed and turned away, murmuring something about not neglecting the guests.

I mingled for a while with the crowd, speaking

to those whom I recognized beneath their finery and welcoming those whom I did not know, complimenting the girls on their varied costumes. The masque was a raging success, if such success could be based on the sound of laughter, the countless plates of food and glasses of wine consumed. As for me, I cared for none of it now, wishing only that they would all disappear and leave me alone with my love. I could feel him, circling the room as I did, and his presence seemed to fill the house, covering me with warmth.

The mention of my name and a burst of laughter caught my attention and I walked over to the corner where Monique was still deep in conversation with two of the guests. I wrapped my arm around her waist and gave her a kiss. "Having a good time, little lamb?"

"Max," I said, nodding to the monk, and "Victor," to the death's head, "I see you have managed to entertain Monique in my absence."

"Quite the contrary, Vivienne," Victor said, "she was entertaining us. I see that some of your, ah, charm, has worn off on her. She is a delightful companion."

I nodded. "I am glad you approve, Victor. And, Max?" I gave him a warning look. "What do you have to say?"

He laughed. "Well, she is a vast improvement over your last pick. You will get no interference from me at this point, but I think you may be moving too quickly."

I laughed back at him and rolled my eyes. This from the man who had given me only one last sunrise? "What little patience I have, Max, I learned from the master. But I am as sure of her as I can be."

Monique looked back and forth at the three of us while we spoke, her dark eyes searching mine, trying to gather some meaning out of our cryptic conversation. "Vivienne? I don't understand. Have I done something wrong? Offended anyone?"

"No, of course not, little lamb. Do not let these gentlemen intimidate you, Monique. You are wonderful and will continue to be so."

"Good. I see that Eduard is here."

I ducked my head to hide my smile of pure pleasure; instinct told me that my romance with Eduard should be kept hidden from both Max and Victor. "Yes, of course he is here. Are we not the most fashionable house in all of Paris?"

"But you have left him alone. Shall I go and keep him company?"

"I am sure he would enjoy your company, Monique. Tell him I will be along presently."

She nodded, curtsied prettily to Max and Victor, picked up two glasses of red wine from the closest tray, and moved across the room. I watched her navigate her way through the crowd to reach him, looked at the two of them standing close together, his blond head bending close to her dark one. Holding my breath and biting my lip, I tried to hide the violent flash of jealousy I felt as he brought her hand up to his mouth. Monique smiled up into his face and I clenched my jaws and fists.

"I presume that this Eduard is a special friend of yours, Vivienne. I would like to meet him." In the time I had been watching the dancers, Victor seemed to have vanished, but Max had remained by my side. His voice was a strange mix of concern, curiosity, and suspicion. When he offered me a glass of wine, I relaxed my hand, smiled my thanks, and took a sip. "He seems familiar to me, somehow. Perhaps he and I have met before?"

"I would not think so, Max. *Mon chou,* he is just a man, nothing remarkable or memorable."

"Ah. A regular of the house then?"

"No, not exactly." I took another sip of the wine to cover my nervousness. "He is a doctor, you see. Monique brought him here to tend to Rosa the night she died."

"Wait! Rosa is dead? When did this happen and why didn't you tell me?"

I shrugged, my eyes darting back over to where they stood talking. Monique was laughing and Eduard was touching her elbow and leading her out to the dance floor.

"Vivienne?"

"Hmmm?" I could almost feel the weight of his hand on her waist.

"We were speaking of Rosa. And how she came to be dead."

"Yes, we were." She looked happy and dizzy, much the same, I imagine, as I looked when dancing with the man.

Max reached over and gave my shoulder a shake. "Wake up, girl, what is wrong with you this evening?"

With great effort, I turned my back on the dancers and poured my full attention into the conversation. "Rosa got sick one day a while ago. Monique went to fetch the midwife; she's quite skilled, you know, even with situations other than childbirth. But Marie was out on another call. And Eduard happened to be walking by, heard Monique inquire after her, and volunteered his services."

"How fortunate for Monique." His voice acquired an edge and I shivered. "But he didn't seem to do much to help Rosa, did he?"

"He did the best he could, Max. He explained to me that the poison was too firmly entrenched in her system and that he could not do anything to check it."

"Poison?" His voice rose over the noise of the room and several people nearby turned and stared. Max glared at them, then smiled an evil grimace and motioned with his finger that they were to turn around. Not surprisingly, they obeyed his unspoken command. He lowered his voice. "What do you mean? Rosa was poisoned?"

I gave a small humorless laugh. "That is exactly what I said at the time. But he did not mean that she was poisoned as in someone trying to kill her, just that there was poison in her system. His best theory was that she had eaten some tainted meat or other food. And, well, the food supply has been rather unreliable lately, or so I have heard. There seems to be no shortage of blood, at least."

"True."

"I am sure he was right about the food, Max. Why would he lie to me?"

"Why, indeed." He took a drink of his wine and watched the dance floor. "The tainted food theory seems rather likely, as much as I hate to admit it. And Rosa was not immortal and was getting old. Still, I don't like the thoughts of you being unprotected."

"But Monique protects me now."

"I see. And so Monique is now filling Rosa's position? Once again, how fortunate for her."

I knew what he was implying and I grew angry. He had started out this way with Diego and I was determined that not happen again. "Listen to me, Max, you black-hearted bastard." I stared deeply into his eyes and did not relent. "This one has nothing to do with you, do you understand? Diego and I were living under your roof and your protection when you murdered him, so perhaps your actions were proper. But this house is my territory; it has nothing to do with you and you will not interfere. Do you hear me? You will not interfere; I will not allow it."

Max looked away first and I counted that a victory. "Very well, Vivienne," he said, sounding penitent, although not one bit less arrogant. "Let us call a truce and discuss it no more."

I smiled, placated by his tone; he couldn't help his arrogance any more than I could. It was part and parcel of what we were. The knowledge of our superiority over humans carried into every one of our interactions. "Yes, let us change the topic. How are you enjoying the party?"

He gave a grunt. "Like any large gathering of humans, it makes me nervous. And hungry. But I have to say"—and he got a mischievous glint in his eye—"this hat object you are wearing is making me crazy."

I giggled. "You are right, Max, as always." Reaching up, I slid the headdress and the wig off, setting it down on the table as if it were a platter of food. Pulling the pins out of my hair, I tossed my head and combed out the tangles with my fingers. "Ah, that feels so much better. And if the truth be known, Max, that headdress is one of the worst mistakes I have ever made."

His eyes strayed to the dance floor; the music had ended and Monique and Eduard were making their way over to us. "I doubt that, my dear, but I think it would be wise of me to leave now. I will perhaps get to meet the inestimable Eduard another night. In fact, I will make an effort to do exactly that." He bowed to me and quickly slipped away into the crowd, before I could comment or even say good night.

No matter. Eduard was back. And once again the rest of the guests seemed to disappear. I took his hand.

"I see," he said, "that Mademoiselle Cygnette has lost her head."

"Hush," I said to him, "that is not a good thing to say out loud. And it is not my head that I have lost."

"What then?"

I put a finger to his lips. "Hush," I said again and started to lead him out of the room, "and come with me. I grow weary of this celebration."

He smiled at me and I lost myself in his eyes. "Bored with your own masquerade, Vivienne? What shall we do to remedy that?"

"I am not sure, Monsieur le Docteur, but I feel confident we will find something to do."

Thirteen

"I have always meant to ask you," Eduard said as we entered the door to my room, "about this wooden chest at the foot of your bed."

"What is there to know?" I laughed and came up behind him, putting my arms around his waist and resting my head on his shoulder. "It is a chest. It is wooden. And"—I flung my hand out—"voilà! It is at the foot of my bed."

"But what purpose does it serve? It has no lock on it, so you must not use it for valuables. I have never seen you put anything into it. Or take anything out of it, for that matter." He reached over and lifted the lid before I could stop him.

"We store linens in it," I said, darting around and slamming the lid. I sat down on top of it and kicked my legs back and forth.

"But," he said, reaching down and picking me up, "not very many linens, as far as I could see. The lid felt so heavy, it must be made of something more than just wood. And why is the lock on the inside?"

"Because, my dearest Eduard, that is where the lock is. Why ask me? I did not make the silly box.

It is, if you must know, a family heirloom. And"—I twisted in his arms, wrapped my feathered wings tightly around him, and looked deep into his eyes—"I do not wish to discuss it. Now, make love to me, *mon cher,* so that I do not regret missing my own celebration."

He smiled at me and kissed my forehead. "We would not want you to regret a thing, Vivienne. It would age you. And even you must beware of the passages of time."

"Even I?" I smiled as he carried me to the bed and laid me down gently, as if I were made of porcelain.

"Foo." I snapped my fingers. "I will never grow old." Then I pulled him down to me. "At least as long as you are here."

His mouth fell on mine and once again I lost myself in his embrace. Like the first time, I thought that moments like these were ones for which I would gladly die.

And then I ceased to think. And gave myself over to emotion and touch.

"Vivienne?"

"Hmmm?"

"Although you seem to plan on living forever, I fear I may not be here all that much longer."

"Nonsense, my sweet man." I ran my nails down his arm and laughed at his shivers. "The night is still young."

Eduard sighed. "No, you do not understand. I have reason to believe that I will soon be a prisoner of the revolution. As physician to some of the royal family I have been rather too outspoken in my dislike of the unruly mob that now rules Paris."

"What?" I sat straight up in bed and stared down at him. "And you have been so careful to warn me away from just such a situation. How do you know?"

He nodded. "I know. It is one of the reasons I tried to stay away from you. I would not want to lead the mob here to your house."

"I do not care one bit for the mob. But if you feel you are in danger, we must make arrangements for you to leave the city. No, leave the country entirely. I have friends who . . ."

My voice trailed off. I had exactly two friends who were in the position to offer succor, and somehow I did not think either one of them would welcome me if accompanied by my current paramour.

Nor did I wish to put Eduard in danger. Diego had been miles and even decades away from a guillotine and still he had lost his head.

"No." He pulled me back down to him. "I should not even have mentioned it. I hadn't meant to. But," and he sighed again and whispered his words into my neck, "I did not want to go without saying good-bye. You have made such a difference to my life in such a short time and I hope you will remember me fondly after I am . . ."

I silenced him with a kiss. "No talk of death, Eduard. Here, in my room, in my house, there is no death for you. I will not allow it. And what if there were a way to hold death at bay? Would you take immortality if it were offered?"

"Perhaps," he said, his voice growing distant,

"that is what I am doing. You are right, though, we should not be talking of this." He looked into my eyes and stroked my hair. "You are to forget that I have said anything, my dear. I am being morose, as I am wont to be at times. It means nothing; I have had premonitions all my life and I am still here, still alive."

I curled up next to him, running my nails lazily down his chest and to his groin. I giggled at his instant reaction to my touch. "Wonderfully alive, I would say. No." I continued to caress him. "Gloriously alive. And you will stay that way if I have the slightest say in the matter."

Eduard laughed and gave me a long, slow, and passionate kiss. "How could I not, now that you have ordered it? Now, let us ring for a bottle of wine and we shall toast our immortality."

Getting out of bed, I wrapped my dressing gown around me. "There will be no answer to the ring, Eduard, not this evening. Let me get the wine."

I was surprised to find the masque still going on when I arrived at the bottom of the stairs. The musicians had long since departed, but the guests were still drinking and singing and talking and dancing. Many couples could be seen in various stages of lovemaking—most of them guests, as the girls hardly considered this activity recreational. Looking around the room, my only thought was how grateful I was that I had others who would clean up the mess. And that when I awoke the next evening and climbed out of my coffin, life would be back to normal.

No one paid any attention to me as I moved

through the room and took one of the few unopened bottles of wine from the table. I noticed my headdress still sitting there on display, still attached to the wig, but someone had gotten a cleaver from the kitchen and cut off the swan's head.

What an odd thing to do, I thought. Then I surveyed the room and watched the guests for a second or two. They were behaving in the most decadent fashion, many in complete deshabille, flagrantly displaying breasts and organs probably best kept clothed. I gave a low laugh and shook my head. A decapitated swan, and not even a real one at that, was mild compared to what they could be capable of. It wasn't as if I was planning on wearing the silly thing ever again; in fact, if I'd thought of it first, I might have done the same thing.

Even so, it looked so pitiful and it seemed such a mean-spirited thing to do. I thought then of tossing them all out into the street. But no, Eduard was waiting.

I paused outside of Monique's room to make sure that she was asleep; not entirely an altruistic gesture. I didn't want her to have another attack of jealousy because Eduard was in our bed. It sounded as if I hadn't needed to worry. She had someone in there with her, a man. They were talking and I went to move on, having seen enough flagrant displays downstairs. But three steps away I stopped, recognizing the male voice, droning, deep. And her voice carried a degree of fear I had never heard in it before.

"No!" I slammed the bottle I carried to the floor, unmindful of the shattering glass and sticky red wine that showered my feet and legs. The door was locked when I turned the handle, so I gripped it harder and turned it again. This time the knob crumbled in my hand as if it had been made of clay.

Max raised his head away from Monique's neck as I burst into the room. His eyes glowed with an unholy pleasure I knew all too well. Blood dripped from his fangs and he growled at me. "Get out, Vivienne. This has nothing to do with you."

I flew at him, nails extended, putting all of my strength into the leap. "She is not yours," I hissed as I knocked him to the ground and raked his face. "She is not yours and I will not permit you to touch her again."

I held him down, nails at his throat now, and turned my head. "Monique, little lamb, go to my room, stay there, and lock the door. Eduard is there, he will protect you. And Max will threaten you no more."

He couldn't have taken much of her blood since she was able to run from the room. I heard her bare feet slapping against the floor, and her gasp of pain as she hit the remains of the bottle. But still she hurried down the hall and soon I heard the door to my room open, then heard it slam shut.

"Are you quite done?" Max pushed away from me as if I weighed nothing, wiped his hands over his already-healing face.

I shook my head in disgust. "All of Paris to feed on, Max, and you had to choose the one forbidden. Why must you be so perverse? So inhuman?

I should never have let you i his house. I would kill you if I knew how."

He laughed and got to his feet, adjusting the monk's robe, tightening the belt about his waist. "You couldn't kill me even if you knew how. You quite simply don't have the nerve for it."

I bared my teeth at him. "Touch her again and we will see just how much nerve I have."

"Be fair, Vivienne. You were busy with the exquisite Eduard; and I thought 'what difference would it make to her if I claimed Monique?' "

"But there was no need for it to be her. Any woman at the masquerade would have gone with you and fed whatever appetites you wanted fulfilled."

"It is not a matter of appetites, my dear. I don't trust her, not one bit, and neither should you. She was skulking outside your door earlier, did you know that? Nasty little habit, staring in at keyholes."

"I don't believe you."

He laughed. "Of course you don't. You are as enchanted with the lovely Monique as you are with the good doctor. And I wish I knew why. It worries me; neither of these humans"—he spat the word—"should be able to exert such power over someone like you."

"You are welcome to your worries, Max, but do not inflict them upon me. And perhaps what is happening is not what you think. Could it not be possible that the great Maximillian Esteban is wrong?"

"Sarcasm does not become you, my dear. It makes you quite unattractive."

"Je m'en fous! I think that the influence Eduard

and Monique have over me has nothing at all to do with power."

"Then what, Vivienne?" He smiled and I wanted to tear into his face again. Instead, I looked away from him.

"Perhaps, Max, this power is love. The truth is that I truly care for the both of them, something a cold bastard like you could never understand."

He threw his head back and laughed. "Love? Now I am even more worried. Did you never listen? What have Victor and I told you time and time again about the false emotion of love?"

I folded my arms and glared at him stubbornly. "It is love, Max, no matter what you think."

He shook his head. "Mark my words, Vivienne, between the two of them, they will have you dead yet. Take care who you give your heart to, lest they tear it out and devour it." He reached over and patted my cheek; I pulled away with a growl. "I have invested a goodly amount of money, time, and blood in you and I do not wish to see it all go for naught."

"I am not your child anymore, Max. And I am not your wife, nor your servant. As far as your investment?" I threw my hands up into the air in exasperation. "I care nothing for that. And if the truth be told, neither do you. All you wish is to have total control over me and mine. And that will not happen. I do not wish to see you ever again. Please do not return."

He shrugged. "As you wish. But my offer for safe haven still applies. I would welcome you should you need a place to go. Blood binds us together more thoroughly than ever love would."

"I will seek sanctuary with you, Max, when I'm dead and buried."

He laughed. "Technically, of course, you already are dead, but we won't argue over semantics now." He nodded, bowed with a flourish, and walked out the door, his boots crunching on broken glass.

Fourteen

When I got back to my room, I knocked softly on the door. Eduard flung it open with a questioning look. "What exactly is happening here, Vivienne? She's been bitten, not by any sort of animal I am familiar with. And her feet are all bloody."

I sighed and glanced over to where Monique lay, sobbing and gasping for breath on the lounge, holding a red-stained cloth to the open wound on her neck. The air was full of the tang of blood; I caught my breath and walked over to her, kneeling down and brushing her hair back from her pale face.

"Did she tell you what happened?" I asked, giving Eduard a quick glance out of the corner of my eyes, before turning my attention back to Monique. I moved her hand away from the cloth and tucked it down at her side, peering underneath to see the damage. Max had not just bitten her, he'd worried at the wound like a mad dog. "Bastard," I whispered under my breath. "I should have killed him where he stood."

She smiled up at me weakly. "I am all right, Vivienne. You saved me. Again. Thank you."

"Poor little lamb, I am so sorry. This should not have happened."

"What should not have happened? What exactly is going on here?" Eduard raised his voice and both Monique and I jumped.

"Oh, hush," I said, "you are upsetting her more. Bring me some of the brandy on the night table and a glass."

He nodded and did as I asked.

I laughed as I put the glass up to her lips and she choked a bit on the bitter drink. "I seemed destined to force brandy on you, my lamb. Drink it all up, yes, that's a good girl." I filled another one. "One more and then we will have the doctor look at your feet."

After the second brandy, she fell asleep and Eduard was able to pick out the bits of glass that had imbedded themselves in the soles of her feet. He washed them and bandaged them; left her to sleep on the lounge with one of the blankets from my bed to cover her. Eduard fussed a bit more over the wound on her neck, but I knew it would heal well.

"Thank you," I said. "I could have managed, but you were much gentler and thorough than I would have been."

"Of course," he said, "but now will you please tell me what happened?"

"One of our guests got a little carried away in his merriment. I have seen to it that he will not return."

"And her feet? What happened there? They were cut to ribbons. She won't be able to walk for weeks."

"That, I fear, is my doing. I dropped the bottle

of wine I'd been bringing back for us and she ran through it on her way here. Nothing more hideous than that."

"Ah." He gave me a smile. "I didn't mean to yell at you or blame you. I was merely worried for the girl. I am sorry, though, that my request for wine ended this way."

I gave him a wan smile. "Actually, if you hadn't sent me out for drink, it might have been worse." I shivered slightly. Would Max have drained her dry? Torn her apart? Left her dead body for me to find or tossed her into the streets? "But it was not the worst and she'll be fine in a day or two. Thank you again."

He shook his head. "I can't help but think that there is more to the situation than you are telling me. But as no lasting harm was done, I will trust your explanations. And your assurance that this will not happen again."

"I will do everything I can to protect her, as I have since she arrived here."

"Good."

An awkward silence fell on us. For me, I was ever aware of the impending sunrise and Eduard was distant, distracted.

"I do think that I should be—"

"It has been wonderful—"

We both spoke at the same time and laughed nervously.

"Ladies first," he finally said.

"I am glad you came back." It was as close as I could get to saying what I really wanted to say. The words of love, the words that told how empty I felt in his absence, how much I missed his voice, his touch when he was gone—these words froze up in my throat. All I could do was smile. And say it again. "So very glad, Eduard."

"As am I."

He gathered me up into his arms and held me, swaying slightly. I turned my head to draw in the delicious scent of him and moved my mouth onto his neck, not to feed, not to bite, but to savor his taste. And as I nuzzled, he kept me close, stroking my hair, rocking us both gently back and forth. Tears began to stream down my face; I hadn't cried a tear since the night Max transformed me. I turned my face away and wiped my eyes on my dressing gown sleeve, sniffed once, and pulled out of his arms.

Nothing more needed to be said. He picked up his fool's cap from the bedpost, kissed me once on the forehead, and walked out the door. I smiled, even as I continued to cry, listening to the jangling sound of his costume's bells until he was gone.

Eduard never returned. For a few weeks he sent letters daily, tied with red satin ribbons onto bundles of violets and lavender. Monique reported that she would sometimes see him in passing on the streets when she ventured out. He never spoke to her, she said, never even looked her in the eye. "Perhaps he didn't see me. I could follow him the next time if you'd like."

"No, Monique. He knows where I am, knows that I am waiting. Do not seek him out. There is no need."

But there was a need, and it was my need, one stronger than I ever would have believed. The tears I had cried that last evening were a response to the truth—somehow I had known, even without his talk of fate and death, that he would leave and I would never see him again.

I grew moody and temperamental, withdrawing more into the shell I had occupied before he arrived. I rarely left my room, and when I did come out I remained veiled and did not speak to anyone. Monique faithfully escorted a patron of the house to my room every few nights and I would feed halfheartedly.

These feedings involved no real contact—no touch, no loveplay, not even the delicious rush of power I often felt flowing through me with the blood. I would take what little I needed, impart the suggestion that the victim should forget, and send him on his way.

During the day, I would lie in my wooden box, surrounded by the dying flowers he had sent, grasping his letters in my hands as if they alone kept me alive. I tried not to sleep, since dreams of him were torture, so vivid and real I often felt that all I needed to do was roll over and open my eyes and there he would be. In those dreams, he was with me and I could reach over and feel him next to me, taste his blood, touch the silklike texture of his skin, thrill to the brush of his lips on mine.

At night I had taken to standing, naked and in total darkness, in front of an open window, curtains pulled back and shutters thrown wide open. I searched the face of everyone who passed below my window, hoping beyond hope that this one would be Eduard. It never was. But as their footsteps receded, I would close my eyes to wait for the approaching steps of another, praying to the God I had abandoned with my mother's death, praying for the return of love. Each time I looked I found only strangers, and in truth I did not expect different, yet I could not help myself.

I was empty now, without him. Emptier than I had been before we met, because I knew now what I lacked. I knew that he was out in the city, somewhere; I perceived his presence as tangibly as the kiss of the night breeze on my naked skin.

Night after night I stood thus, searching, hoping, and praying until dawn threatened. Then Monique would take me by the hand and pull me away from the window, closing it tightly against the sun. Clothing me in a white satin nightdress, she would brush my hair and wash my face and hands, leading me eventually to the wooden chest at the foot of the bed so that I could once again spend the day with his letters and his flowers.

Had it not been for Monique, I'd have ended as one of the fatalities of which Max and Victor had spoken. My life rested in her hands during these days and nights and she more than repaid my trust in her as she had more than disproved Max's suspicions.

Max's suspicions did not matter now, for Max had disappeared as completely as Eduard had, taking Victor with him, I presumed. All I had left in the world was Monique.

I felt sorry for myself for a little over a month. Then, one evening, as I came out of my coffin, I noticed a difference in my emotions, a lightening of my spirits. And any discomforting dreams I might have experienced must have faded upon wakening exactly as dreams should, for they left no pieces of themselves behind.

I stretched and yawned; my sleep had been deep and nourishing. Why should it not have been? Hadn't it always been so? For a long moment I could not remember why I had been unhappy, only that I had been. And now, I was not. Something had changed.

Thinking, I stretched again and realized, with a girlish laugh—*the hurt is gone.* It was not that I had stopped loving Eduard; I did still and feared that love would be with me always. But the sharp ache of missing him wasn't there. I sat on a little chair in front of the mirror and brushed my hair, humming a song I'd heard someone singing outside my window years ago. Smiling at my image, I leaned over and kissed it. "I am back," I said with a giggle, "and I am very hungry. But oh, I feel wonderful."

"You do?" The mirror reflected the occupant of the bed as she poked her head out from underneath the covers.

"Yes, I do, *mon chou.* And why shouldn't I?"

Monique got up and stood behind me, taking the brush from my hand. "And that was my thought always. I am glad you've come around. I was worried."

I peered at her reflection in the mirror as she brushed my hair. She did indeed look worried. Her skin was sallow and lifeless and her eyes were rimmed by dark circles, as if she too had been unable to sleep. As I looked closer I saw that she had been crying.

I pulled her hand down to my mouth and kissed it. "You are a sweet little lamb, Monique. And I will always be grateful to you. Just remember." I gave her hand a little playful nip. "Next time you swear you hate me and wish me dead, remember that you could have destroyed me at any time this past month and I would not have been able to stop you."

She smiled. "I am already regretting it."

"Foo," I said with another laugh, "you love me and you know it. Just as I love you."

"What about Eduard? We have to talk about him, Vivienne."

I made a face in the mirror and stuck my tongue out at her. "Nothing to talk of. Eduard is gone." I felt her tremble. Had she disliked him so much? "And whatever enchantment he held over me is gone with him."

She continued brushing my hair, smoothing and stroking. It felt so good to have her do this; it felt so good not to hurt as I had. I gave a long, low hum of pleasure and Monique smiled and kissed the top of my head.

"And so, Monique, you have been pretty much cooped up in this room with me for over a month. Shall I give you the night off?"

She started to protest, but I continued.

"Or would you like to come hunting with me? You have asked for me to give you this gift of immortality and yet you have no idea what it entails. Coming out with me would be good preparation for your soon-to-be new life."

She clapped her hands together. "That is certainly an easy choice, Vivienne. Hunting, of course! What should I wear? Where will we be going?"

"Let's just walk for a while. Wear something

dark, so that we are not so obvious, and I will show you a side of Paris you have never seen before."

We set off, arm in arm, looking nothing more than two ladies taking a leisurely stroll. In a low voice, I began explaining to Monique what to look for in a victim. "Never choose one too old or too young."

"The blood isn't as good?"

I laughed, drawing a curious look from a few passersby. "Not at all. Blood is blood. Even the blood of animals will sustain us for a while. And while it is true that everyone's blood carries a different taste, a different feel, I have never tasted any that was bad. But taking from the very old and the very young is risky since they are most likely to suffer ill effects from our feeding. They could sicken. Or die."

"And what difference does that make? You are superior to humans in every way. Why should you care? And when I am like you, why should I care?"

I stopped and pulled back from her so that I could look her in the face. "It makes all the difference in the world, my lamb. A vampire who kills repeatedly is one who eventually will be discovered and killed herself. You take what you need, no more. Survival. It is the first lesson Max taught me. And perhaps the most important. Never call attention to what you are, never let them know you are there, waiting. And never let them remember."

"You call attention to yourself. Most of Paris knows who you are."

"Ah, that may be true. But do they know what I am?"

She thought for a moment as we walked on. "No, I don't believe they do. And if they did, what then?"

I sighed. "I would be hunted down and killed. Have no doubts on that count. Superstitions still rule the common people. I am, as you may have noticed, an evil creature, a minion of Satan himself, if you would believe the priests."

"The priests are wrong." She smiled. "You have many faults, it is true, but you are not evil."

We turned down the next street and walked along the river for a time, all the while moving slowly and certainly toward Place du Carroussel.

"The priests may be wrong, but that does not stop their followers from listening. Wrong is not always visible from outside appearances. You know this, we all know this." I made a sound of disgust and spat on the ground. "Pah! We would live in a better world without the priests and the leaders telling us what we should do and how we should live."

We continued walking in silence for a while. The streets seemed ominously empty; most respectable people would be home with family. And the reprobates would undoubtedly avoid this square like the plague. But I was neither and there was something on display here I wanted to see. Something that defined this time and this city. I should have come before and I would have, despite my confessions of disinterest, had I not been distracted by Eduard.

"But I don't understand," Monique said, "you may scoff all you like, but you *could* make it better.

With all your powers, all your strength, you could rule the world."

I laughed even harder, and my high-pitched voice echoed down the narrow streets, sounding furtive and guilty. No doubt it was the first laughter this spot in Paris had heard for some time.

Monique looked angry at my laughter. "You could rule the world," she repeated like a child. "You should rule the world."

"Rule the world? Why would anyone want such a task? You, my lamb, are living in times that prove such ambitions vain. And deadly."

She noticed, at last, where we were standing. Even in the darkness, I could tell that she'd gone paler. The wooden platform smelled of newly hewn wood. And fear. And blood.

"Here, Monique, this is the fate of those who wish to rule. For me, I wish no part of it. Nor would I wish it on any."

She shivered next to me as we stood looking at the handiwork of mankind.

Fifteen

"Why are we here?" Monique whispered.

"A good question, my pretty ladies." A guard came out of the shadows of one of the walls. "There is nothing to see here right now. Just wood and steel, and"—he took a long look at us and made an effort to stand taller in his uniform—"myself." He stepped closer and smiled, stroking his mustache and beard. "And I am, of course, your obedient servant."

I glanced at Monique, nodding my head ever so slightly in the guard's direction. "Watch me." I mouthed the words and she flashed a quick understanding smile.

"Good evening, *mon Capitaine.* And just how obedient a servant are you, I wonder?"

He picked up on the sexual invitation my voice offered and smirked, putting his hand over his heart and bowing. "Obedient enough, pretty one, and more than willing to serve your every need."

I laughed and slowly moved closer to him, so close that I could smell the cheap wine he had been drinking. Looking into his eyes, I lowered the pitch of my voice. "You sound so sure of yourself. I like that in a man. But how shall I test your sincerity?"

"Give me a task, lady, so that I can prove myself worthy of your attentions."

I nodded and paused, as if thinking of a task, while he stood expectantly in front of me awaiting my command. *So very easy,* I thought, *there is no challenge here. He is already mine.*

"Would you, perhaps, explain to me how this machine works? I have heard so much about it, but alas, have not been able to see it demonstrated."

"It is quite simple, lady. The traitor mounts the stairs and lays his head on the platform, the lunette. The executioner pulls the lever, the *declic,* and whoosh!" He made a chopping motion with his hand against his other wrist. "It is done. The leather bag that had held the heads has now been replaced with a basket of sorts." He laughed and shot me a sly smile. "Although not the sort of thing a pretty mademoiselle would want to take to market."

"Have you done this? Have you pulled the lever and watched the blade fall?"

"Me? No. We have Sanson for the task. He is quite skilled. In fact, he was here today for the newest list. You should have come to witness the event—many of the city's fine ladies do. Today the list was long. And still the number of traitors to our glorious revolution grows."

"No doubt. And who was on this list? Can you tell me that?"

I really didn't care to know, I was not even sure why I had asked. And I knew what his answer would be.

"No, I fear I could not tell you that, even if I remembered."

"Then, perhaps, you are not as obedient as you promised."

He shook his head and put his arms out in a supplicating gesture. "But surely, lady, you can find a more appropriate task for me. Why do you care for the names of the traitors?"

"I do not, that is true." I looked over at Monique where she had sat down on the steps of the platform. She was staring at the steel blade fixed in its upright position, holding her arms to herself and shivering despite the warmth of the night. "What do you think," I asked her, "shall we forgive this good soldier and give him a kiss good night?"

She stood up and came over to us. "Yes," she said, "and then let us go. I don't like it here."

The guard looked back and forth at the two of us. "Kisses from two such beautiful ladies would make this night duty a pleasure. Who shall be first: the raven-haired one who is hauntingly familiar in her beauty or the blond goddess?"

I laughed. "Save me for last, *mon Capitaine,* I am likely to leave you too exhausted for kissing anyone else afterward."

He turned to Monique and kissed her, a perfunctory gesture. She stood stiffly and accepted his attentions. *We will have to work on that,* I thought, *she must not be unwelcoming. But there is time and she is not yet a vampire.*

"My turn." I opened my arms and the guard fell into them, his lips on mine before I could move. Although his obedience was in question, his aggression certainly made up for the lack. I pushed away from him. "Slowly, lover, you needn't be in such a hurry."

"Ah," he said, groaning, his hands grasping at my waist and pulling me to him, "but you taste so good I need more than one kiss."

I laughed softly. "Here? In front of this damnable machine? I think not, my good Captain."

"No?"

"No. We bargained for kisses and kisses are all you will get. But I promise you will not regret them."

And now I turned the aggressor. I kissed his mouth, hard and hurried, pulling at his lower lip with my teeth, grazing him for that first delicious taste of blood. He lifted me toward him and I wrapped my legs around his waist, still kissing him, nuzzling the skin of his cheeks, giving a low purr of delight. "Perhaps," I whispered huskily, "for such a strong and handsome soldier I can give a little more than kisses."

I felt him throb up against me in response and as his hands traveled under my skirts and up to my thighs, I took advantage of his distraction and fastened my mouth on his neck.

How fortunate that he was so strong and so hungry for a woman. When I bit him, he didn't drop me, nor did he flinch or fight. Instead he leaned farther into me, holding me tightly, letting my teeth sink deep into his flesh. I drew on him, enjoying the hot rush of his blood on my tongue and in my throat. Each swallow burned into my body, filling me, burning in its wake all fears and aches and thoughts of lost love. None of that mattered; all that remained was my mouth and my hunger and the satisfaction of blood.

As always, when I drank of my victims' physical substance, I concentrated on their spiritual aspects as well, capturing a bit of their personality and essence to carry with me into eternity, my way of paying them back for their sacrifice. I found in his mind the image of a girl he had loved who had died giving birth to his first child. I saw the child too, dying of a fever in his arms. His mind and his life were opened to me in the feeding and I kept what I could to hold for him.

The grasp he had on my waist began to falter, so I slid my legs down and stood on the ground, still drinking at his neck, but more slowly now, like the gentle, weary touch after the frenzy of love. Then, with a sigh from both of us, I pulled away.

"Forget," I whispered in his ear. "This never happened. I do not exist, except in your dreams. You have fallen asleep while on duty again." Leading him back to the post he had been standing when we arrived, I kissed his cheek. "Thank you, *mon Capitaine.* Sleep now. And wake up with no memory of me." He lay down, curled up, and was softly snoring even before I could turn away.

I wiped my mouth with the back of my hand and looked for Monique. She was standing on the platform now, staring up at the *mouton.* The blade shimmered faintly in the moonlight, blood tinged, although that may have just been a reflection from the red painted wood surrounding it. She caressed the wooden framework, running her fingers over it as if it were a lover's skin, her lips moving as if in prayer. Then she leaned over and kissed what the guard had called the lunette.

"Monique?"

Although I said her name softly, she reacted as if I had screamed it across the square. She jumped and shivered, turning unfocused eyes on me.

"Monique?" I said it again, this time with more command. "Come down from there, lamb, I would not want the rope to shift."

She shook herself slightly as if awakening and looked around her in confusion. "What am I doing up here?"

"A good question. And one I was just about to ask."

"I don't know; it was like a dream. I felt something pulling me to this spot." She shivered and hurried down the platform stairs. "Are you finished with the guard already? I fear I wasn't watching all that closely."

I shrugged. "Do not fret about it, my lamb. There will be other feedings and other nights. You have many years in which to learn the art."

"So, did he finally tell you who was executed today?"

"No. It does not matter."

"But I want to see if you can make him tell you. He must know the names and you should be able to drag them out of him. Try. Please. Show me how this control of one's victims is done."

I nodded. "Fine, if you wish." I walked back over to the guard and knelt down next to him. "Listen to me, *mon cher,* while you still sleep, I want you to tell me the names of those executed today."

He muttered something.

"Louder, *mon Capitaine,* so that I can hear."

He began to rattle off a list of names, meaningless to me since this was merely a demonstration of my power. I barely listened as he gave names, professions. I motioned to Monique. "Let's go now, while he is still reciting . . ."

As I started to go, I heard a name that chilled me and I turned back to him. "Stop. Say that last name again, if you please."

He paused, trying to remember what that last name was. Then, without emotion, without remorse, he said what I had dreaded to hear.

"Eduard DeRouchard, Physician to the Royal Family."

Sixteen

"You knew!"

We had walked back to the House of the Swan in silence. Each step I took fed my rage, so that by the time I closed and locked the door to my room my temper was totally out of control.

She said nothing in reply, had no defenses, no prepared alibi to stave off my wrath.

"You knew, you lying bitch!" I screamed the words, totally uncaring of who heard. "You had to have known, otherwise you'd not have had me ask the guard for the names. Is that true?"

Still silent, she met my eyes and I found that I could read nothing in them. Saw nothing but the reflection of my anger. She should have been frightened. *Why isn't she frightened?* I wondered. *Does she not know I hold her life in my hands?*

"Monique? Answer me."

She studied the carpet at her feet. "I don't know what I should say, Mademoiselle. If I say that I am innocent of the foreknowledge of Eduard's death, you would find me guilty anyway."

"So." I walked over to her, grabbed her chin,

and forced her head up so that I could see her eyes, placing the nails of my other hand at her neck, reopening the wound Max had given her. Small trickles of blood began to form and still her eyes held no fear. "Admit it and I will let you live. You did know."

"As you wish."

"That is not an answer, Monique."

"I am sorry, then, for it is the best I can do."

Another thought occurred to me then, with the remembrance of Max's suspicions. She seemed to have hated Eduard. Could it have been possible that she had turned him over to the executioner? And on what charges?

"And perhaps"—my voice grew quiet now, almost a whisper, my nails digging deep gouges into her skin—"perhaps it is more than just the foreknowledge of his death you cannot admit to. Perhaps you had a hand in it."

"No," she wailed, reacting now with a little more vehemence, "whatever you may think of me, Vivienne, do not think that. I loved him too."

Silent tears began to stream down her face, matching the rivulets of blood that flowed down her neck.

"You loved him?"

"Yes, I did." She wiped the tears off her face with her sleeve in an angry gesture. "I did not love him for him. But for your sake."

Suddenly all of my anger rushed out of me. Dropping both of my hands, I pulled her into my embrace and let her cry.

As if the tears had opened a gate, she spoke. "I saw him die, Vivienne. Word was brought here early this morning as you slept that he would be executed."

"You should have woken me."

"With what end? For you to rush out into the broad daylight and die also? No, I could not do that. But I could be a witness for you, so that you would know what happened. He died well, showed no fear of the crowd or the blade." She moved away from me and sat down on the lounge, wiping her tears on her sleeve.

"They were like dogs, that crowd. Howling like dogs for blood. But Eduard faced them, he looked them in the eyes and they backed off like the animals they are." She continued to sob as she talked, sniffling and wiping.

"Did he have anything to say? Somehow I cannot imagine Eduard going without some fine words to be remembered by."

She nodded. "He did, he said 'Good citizens of France, beware the passages of time.' And then as Sanson released the blade, 'I will return.' "

I shook my head. "Good last words, Eduard," I said with a soft laugh at the irony, "but I do not see how you can keep your promise."

"Nevertheless," Monique said, "those were his words." She paused a bit and put her hand up to her neck, noticing in confusion the blood there.

"Ah, let me tend to that for you, *mon chou.* I was angry, but I should not have hurt you like this. You have been hurt enough for one short lifetime." Soaking a handkerchief in the water basin by the bed, I dabbed at the drying blood.

She accepted my ministrations passively, hardly flinching as I cleaned the new and the old wounds.

"I claimed his body." She gulped a bit and sniffed. "And his head."

"What?"

"It did not seem right, to let him lie there with the others. So I told them I was his wife and they let me take him away."

"Why would you do such a thing, Monique? And what did you do with him?"

"I washed him and dressed him in some clean clothes I found here. I"—she gulped again—"I sewed his head back on the best I could. One can hardly tell . . ."

"Where is he?"

"I had them put him in Rosa's room. So that we could have a coffin prepared to bury him properly."

I looked at her in disbelief. "And you did all of this today while I was sleeping? Why did you not tell me when I awoke?"

"I—" She hesitated, pulling in a short breath. "I could not bring myself to say the words, Vivienne. You were so much improved, so much like your old self. I did not want you to go back down into that darkness in which you have been dwelling."

"I understand. And I thank you for your kindness and your care. But can you tell me why you did any of this at all? Why claim his body? Why wash him and dress him and"—I shuddered slightly—"sew him back together?"

She glanced away from me, not meeting my eyes. "So that you could say good-bye."

Monique took me by the hand and led me to Rosa's room as if I did not know the way. It was as she said. Eduard lay there, still and pale. I pulled aside his shirt collar and jabot, peering at the jagged cut and her careful stitching. I still was not sure why she had done this, but I could not deny the truth.

I sighed and leaned over to kiss his cold lips. They held no warmth, no attraction. This was not my Eduard, but rather a husk that he had shed.

I wondered where he had gone, where his charm and determination were now. "Poor Eduard," I said to him, "death has turned you into a liar. You will never return. And I will always miss you."

Somewhere out on the street a dog barked and a baby cried. Monique shivered and hugged her arms to herself. "I asked around and found out that his family has a crypt. His brothers will come for him tomorrow and he will be laid to rest there."

I nodded. "Thank you. It's good that I was able to see him; I'd never have been able to imagine him dead otherwise."

"After everything you have done for me, Vivienne, it's a small thing."

I shrugged. "Quite to the contrary, my lamb, I'd say it was a Herculean task you've accomplished. I doubt that I shall ever be able to repay you."

We stood in silence for a while and all I could think about was the futility of human life. This man had been gifted when alive; he saved lives, he changed lives, he created objects of beauty, he loved. He was capable of giving a creature like me, damned and unnatural, a chance to love. And now he was gone, taking with him all those unique things that made him who he was.

"Such a waste. The fool man. He did not need to die. I would have saved him from this fate; he had only to ask."

"Oui."

This was why one didn't fall in love, I thought. Eventually they die. Eduard's death happened sooner than I would have expected and under more violent circumstances, but even at that his years had always been limited. I looked over at Monique. *And here is another I love who will die, as certainly as the sun rising.*

"Unless," I said softly, "unless I hold back the dawn for her forever."

"Pardon?"

"Prepare yourself, Monique. I have lost enough loved ones to last me through eternity. I will not lose you. And I will not wait another day. Come."

Seventeen

It was fortunate that I had fed well earlier in the evening. Creating a new vampire was an energy-draining process, as I knew from the one time I had attempted the task. At least this time, I could do what I needed to do without having to worry about the interference of Max.

Monique seemed nervous about the change, which was more than understandable. It was a big step, even for someone who wanted the transformation as much as she seemed to.

"You needn't go through with this, little lamb, if you don't want to. I won't force you. It must be something entered into of your own free will."

"It is," she said. "This is what I want. But"—she gave a little smile—"I can still be frightened, can't I?"

I laughed. "You have no need to be frightened of me, Monique. And I will be gentle, my girl, much more so than Max was with me. You may even find it enjoyable. It is a little like falling asleep and waking up in a wonderful new dream that will never end. And you will never be sick and you will never die."

"How is it done?"

"It is a simple transfer of blood. I take most of yours and replace it with about half of mine. Which leaves us both a little weak for a day or two, until we can feed enough to replenish what we've lost. Within a day or two, you will be completely adjusted to the change."

She smiled wanly. "I do not know, Vivienne. I give you all of my blood and you only give me half back? It sounds like you get the better of the deal."

"Perhaps. I hadn't ever thought of it in that way."

I began to undress. As well as being tiring, creating a new vampire often caused a mess and I didn't want to ruin my dress with bloodstains. She came up behind me and undid the back of my bodice.

"Now," I said as I slid out of the dress and out of the corset and petticoats, "are you sure you really want to go through with this? I feel like I am rushing you. There needn't be a hurry, you are still young and healthy. Rosa hesitated too long; in fact she was still deliberating when she died. But you have years and years before you reach her age."

She gave a choked laugh. "I do not want to reach her age. And besides, that was Rosa. I'm not Rosa and I am sure. What, after all, is there not to like? You love your life, you say so all the time. And you have no regrets."

"True. Then if you have made up your mind, there is no reason to wait. Let's get on with it, we are quickly running out of night."

I sat down on the bed and patted the surface

next to me, smiling. "Take off your clothes, my lamb, then come and"—I gave a small chuckle—"lie down with the lion."

She obeyed and stripped quickly, climbing in and lying down. For a while, we just lay side by side with me stroking her hair and her face, whispering soothing words until I could feel the tenseness of her body relax. I pulled her in closer to me and positioned her with her back facing me. Her body was warm, so soft and alive next to mine, something that I would miss when this night was finished.

I sighed and brushed her hair aside, wrapping an arm tightly about her waist.

"Try not to fight, Monique, if you can. No matter how close to death you feel you are coming, do not fight. And do not fear, I will not let you go."

She nodded. "I will try."

I began kissing her, starting with the corner of her mouth that I could reach, whispering sweet nonsense to keep her calm. I ran my mouth across her cheek and to her ear, then nuzzled my way down to her neck, pulling just a bit on the skin, nipping, testing. The arm that was around her waist I moved up so that my hand cupped her left breast. Her nipple hardened at my touch, a touch that served a triple purpose, to both comfort and distract her and, more importantly, to monitor the beating of her heart.

Still mouthing and licking her soft spice-scented skin, I tightened my grip on her just a bit. She moaned and pressed herself back against me and in one sudden movement, I sank my fangs into her.

Monique tensed against the sharp pain, then relaxed as I drew on her, quicker than I would for a normal feed. I opened my eyes as I drank, watching the color of her skin lighten and pale. The warmth of her body began to transfer to mine as I swallowed more and more of her blood.

She began to shiver and still I drank, pulling almost every available drop out of her. Her heart slowed under my hand, faltered, then restarted, although beating slower with every second. We were past the point of no return now; if I did not replenish her with my blood she would die.

I pulled my mouth away from her neck, shifted my position so that I was kneeling next to her on the bed. Then with one sharpened nail I cut a vertical slash on my wrist. Precious blood spurted out before I could get my arm to her mouth. "Drink, little lamb, drink as much as you can hold."

Max had once told me that this was the critical factor in transformation. There were some, he said, that simply refused to drink. And so they died.

"Drink." I said the word with more command. I would not allow her to die. Not now. Not Monique. I pushed my wrist hard against her mouth. "Drink!"

There was a curious tickling sensation at first as she merely lapped at the flow and I laughed, reaching underneath her now cool body and sitting her up, supporting her back and head. Her lapping grew into hungry swallows and soon she was pulling on me with strength and determination. "That is good, my lamb, keep drinking."

Eventually, I felt myself weaken and pulled my

wrist away from her. Her eyes were squeezed shut like a newborn baby's and she gave a low growl, reaching out greedy hands for me. "No," I said, leaning over to lick a few beads of blood from her lips, "that is enough for now. There will be more later, much more and many laters."

She whimpered a little and I kissed her again. Slowly and deliberately she opened her eyes and looked at me. After studying my face for a long time, she smiled. "Thank you," she said, her voice hoarse and soft. "I feel so alive, and—" She stopped and took a deep breath as she looked all around the room. "Vibrant. And real. It is as if everything were new, and everything were a gift, especially for me." She sprang up from the bed and moved from place to place, pausing first to look out the window, then dashing to the fire to study the flames.

I listened to her exclaim about her heightened awareness, how she could see and hear better than she'd ever thought possible. And how the colors were so very bright and the scents on the night air so fascinating.

"I can smell the flowers in the market stalls, Vivienne." She had run back to the window, thrown open the shutters, and leaned out. "I can smell the flowers," she yelled out into the night and her voice echoed off the surrounding walls. Then she turned around, grinning. "It is as if they are growing right here under our window. Wonderful."

I gave her an indulgent smile and got up from the bed, sliding into my dressing gown and sorting through my armoire for a garment for her. Then I sat back down on the bed and waited. We had, I estimated, only a small amount of time, perhaps only minutes, before dawn. Her euphoria would quickly dissolve in that first encounter with the sun. But I let her have her exuberance knowing there was nothing I could do or say to prepare her for the next shock of her new existence: the object that had once brought light and joy into her young life, as it had to all of us, was an enemy now, to be shunned and avoided at the risk of pain and death.

A harsh lesson, to be sure, but a necessary one. I remembered Max telling me about those new ones who did take the blood, but could not make the adjustment; if left alone they would run out into the sunlight on their very first dawn and thus end both their human life and their vampiric one.

"Oh," Monique said, pulling me out of my thoughts, "you never told me it was like this, Vivienne. Or I'd have begged you sooner to change me." She was standing in front of the mirror, running her hands over her naked body, examining the places where she used to be scarred. Now her skin was like cool porcelain, still a little darker than mine, given her natural complexion. "And I can feel the blood moving through my veins, feeding me, changing me, completing me."

"Wait, little lamb." I walked over to her and handed her a dressing gown. "Put this on. For now, you must dress or you will grow cold in your sleep. There will be plenty of time for you to explore your new body tomorrow evening." I fastened the shutters on the window and pulled the heavy curtains closed. Then I crossed the room and double-bolted the door. "This will have to do, I suppose. But we will need to acquire some human help soon, for guarding and watching and daylight errands."

She nodded, losing some of her elation in the knowledge of what she had become, what she had given up.

"I assume you do not mind sharing my coffin." I opened the lid, shook out the blankets, and fluffed up the cushion, grabbing another from the bed for her. "There's really enough room for two, if we cuddle together. And it is all we have—tomorrow evening we can see about getting you a coffin of your own. But this will be fine for tonight. It will be more than fine. And it is not so bad." I was talking now just to reassure her. Her eyes began to glaze over as the sun moved closer to the horizon. "Yes, tomorrow we will get you your own coffin. But for now, come in with me."

She shivered as my words took effect, watched in silence as I extinguished the candles and climbed into the box. "Come, lamb, it is not so horrible. Trust me when I tell you when the sun rises, you do not wish to be out in the open, no matter how well protected. Come now, it is time. This is the price we pay."

She crawled in next to me and we both lay down. I threw the bolts on the lid, arranged a few blankets over the both of us, and held my breath. Waiting for the dawn.

"This will be a shock to your system, Monique. And there is nothing one can do to prepare for it or prevent it. The rising of the sun is a deadly time for us and our bodies recognize the danger even though our minds know that we are safe. Instinctual reactions, you see. And we have to take the good with the bad."

When dawn came, Monique opened her mouth and a squeaky little gasp escaped her lips. I felt the same shock run through my body, but it was an old sensation for me. For her it was new and frightening and very painful.

"Hush, little one." I pulled her in close to me and whispered into her ear as she sobbed. "It will be all right, you'll see. It does not last long."

Eighteen

Monique slept in my arms that day locked away from the destructive sun, experiencing the first sleep of a vampire—a deep and boneless thing that so closely resembled death that even I, who had experienced it for almost a century, feared that she might have actually died. But no, I could hear the beat of her heart, the rush of her newly transformed blood flowing through her veins. It was a strangely reassuring sound, almost a lullaby, soothing and comforting.

Much more so than the sounds from without.

First there was the knock on the front door, something rare in a house of this nature. Deliveries were made in the back, of course, and most of the working girls would be asleep. No one called during the day. Yet, there was the knock. And someone answered.

I heard deep male voices.

"We are looking for Mademoiselle Courbet. Is she here?"

"She is sleeping, Messieurs, and we all have orders not to disturb her sleep." It was Cecile who had answered the door and I breathed a sigh of relief. She must have been a light sleeper, a fact for which I was grateful now; I felt her capable of handling whatever situation arose.

"I care nothing for your orders," said the man. "I have been told that this house"—the word came out as a sneer—"holds the body of our brother, Eduard DeRouchard."

There was a long pause. I could picture Cecile giving this man her coolest look behind her heavily lidded eyes, assessing not only his worth as a human being but also for his potential as a source of francs. I always pitied the ones who failed either of her tests; they would often mope around for weeks.

This one must have done well, for when Cecile answered there was more of a welcome in her voice than normal. "Yes, Monsieur, he is here. He was your brother? Such a shame, Dr. DeRouchard was a favorite here. Monique had him laid out in Rosa's room."

There was a short barked laugh. "Rosa must be a devoted employee, to entertain a corpse in her room."

"No, Monsieur, you misunderstand me. Rosa is dead also and so—"

He laughed again, interrupting her explanation. "Is this house a mortuary or a brothel?"

"A good question, Monsieur, and one some of us have come to ask."

I tensed. Hopefully she was referring to the number of dead bodies that had been here in the past months and not to the fact that the mistress of the house spent her days sleeping in a coffin. I had no doubts now, this evening I would need to find a watcher for us. And make plans to leave

Paris immediately. My hands began to slide the bolts open, should I need to quickly exit and crawl into the bed. I lay quietly, waiting for the sound of them at my door.

"But if you will follow me, I will show you to Rosa's room. Monique said yesterday that she would prepare the body. I did not know what that entailed, nor did I want to ask. This way, Messieurs."

I heard them mount the stairs and come down the hallway, but they stopped at Rosa's room and entered there.

"Ah, Eduard," the man said. "How glad I am that Mother is not still alive to witness this. It would have broken her heart." He lowered his voice and I thought he was praying, joined by a few of the others. Then his voice grew louder when he, I presumed, addressed the other men in the room. "Go and get the coffin from the cart and bring it up here."

More footsteps down the hall and the stairs and the sound of the door opening.

Cecile gave a little yawn. "Is there anything else you require, Monsieur?"

"No, thank you. You have been quite kind. But we have woken you, have we not? I do apologize for interrupting your rest."

I heard her laugh and thought from the coquettish tone of her voice that Eduard's brother must have been handsome.

"It is no problem, Monsieur, I can sleep when you leave. May I offer you refreshments? I'm not sure what there is in the kitchen, but I would be happy to see."

"No. But thank you. Your name?"

"Cecile."

"A lovely name. I will remember you. Now, my dear, where is this Monique person? I'd like to thank her for the wonderful job she has done. Eduard looks only as if he were sleeping. You have to look closely to see that he is not breathing."

"Yes, he does look quite alive. It will be a comfort for us all to think of him like that."

"Can you get her for me?"

"Who? Monique? She is sleeping in Mademoiselle's room, most likely. Shall I wake her?"

"No."

There was another pause and the sound of feet moving. Cecile giggled. I assumed that he had kissed her or tried to. That he was Eduard's brother there could be no doubt, however inappropriate and irreverent his actions seemed, carrying on a flirtation over the decapitated body of his brother. And for Cecile to giggle as she did, it appeared that not all the charm in the DeRouchard family had been wasted on my dear, dead love. "I seem to have woken enough lovely ladies for the day. Besides, I have an unpleasant task ahead of me. Let the esteemed Monique sleep."

"As you wish, Monsieur."

The other men arrived with much scuffling of feet and a bit of groaning. There was a quiet consultation over how best to get the body into the coffin and then I heard them close the cover.

"Thank you, Cecile. You have been most helpful."

"My pleasure, Monsieur. As I said, Dr. DeRouchard was a favorite of the house. God rest his soul."

There was a low rumble of laughter again. "Yes, well, I suppose that is in God's hands. I couldn't say. Good day."

I heard Cecile sigh and heard them struggle with the coffin on the stairway. The front door opened, then shut. And Eduard, my Eduard, the only man I had ever loved, was gone forever.

I began to cry, silently, holding on to Monique as if she were my only salvation. I cried for Eduard, his life ending like this, abruptly and uselessly. Had I listened to his premonition, had I believed him, I could have stopped this event. We could have gone away, we could have spent eternity together. But I hadn't taken him seriously and so now he was dead.

I cried for Monique, poor little lamb that she was, picturing her claiming the body of a man she hated for the sake of a woman she loved, picturing her washing him and stitching him back together, as if he were a poppet to be mended. I gave a small bitter laugh at the irony of Monique doing all of this for someone such as I. That she loved me did not matter. Of course she did; I had fostered the emotion, mesmerized her with my powers. She had no choice in the matter.

And, in a rare bout of self-pity, I cried for myself, wrapping my limbs about Monique and holding her so closely I could feel her heart beating against mine. I cried for the opportunities of a normal life that I had carelessly and frivolously abandoned. For babies that would never suckle at my breasts. For the joy of growing old with ones that I love. For the sun that I was forever denied.

Then I opened my eyes and wiped away the tears. Ridiculous, that I had been reduced to lying in my coffin crying about situations over which I had no control, grasping for comfort from a wayward girl. This was not the way I usually acted and was certainly not the way I should act.

I needed to remind myself that a creature such as I had no desire for love or for friends; the emotions I experienced with Eduard were nothing but an aberration. It only took the memory of how I had reacted to his desertion to tell me that my love for him was impossible.

And what I had let happen with Monique was more than unfortunate. Now was too soon for her to make the change. She needed months of preparation and guidance, such as I had never received. But I had allowed the desolation and guilt at Eduard's death to make the decision. And there would be repercussions, I knew. As there had been with Diego.

But I would not let Max hurt her. I would not let Max know of her existence. "Don't worry, little one," I whispered to her, "we will go away, away from this horrible city of death. We will hide from those who wish us harm. And I will take care of you as long as you need me to."

Nineteen

"I feel as if I have been starving for years. Hurry. Please."

Monique had awoken very hungry and anxious to try out her newly born powers and senses. I remembered well that excitement and knew that I couldn't really curb it.

"The night is young, little lamb, and we have plenty of time. For now, we need to speak of certain things."

"There is one thing that needs to go," she said, dressing and examining her sharpening teeth in the mirror. "You will have to stop calling me a lamb. Look at my fangs." And she turned and gave me a wicked smile. "Have you ever seen a lamb with such teeth? No, I am a tiger now."

I laughed. "I suppose you are right. But you are not yet a full-grown tiger and you will need to listen to your maman if you wish to survive."

While I dressed, I described to her what I had overheard during the day and outlined the plans I had made. "First thing we must do is find someone to act as our guard. I do not wish to lie awake every day waiting for someone to break down the door. There are enough dangers in this life; and that is one that can be easily avoided. Had I been thinking clearly, I'd have done this task before transforming you."

"Did someone try to break down the door today?"

"No, but it was too close, I thought. I will not permit that to happen again."

"So what sort of person should we choose as our guard? I'd not have been much help to you in any sort of serious confrontation. And neither would Rosa have. Perhaps we should try to find someone more suitable, someone more capable of defending us."

I nodded. "I had never intended for Rosa to serve as my guard as long as she had. But the years piled upon each other and I grew accustomed to the routine we'd established. I have been too careless in the past, counting on the courtesy of those around me. But Cecile showed my how false that courtesy can be. I propose we go back to Place du Carroussel and recruit that guard into a new service. He will do quite well, especially since he is already tied to me."

She nodded. "He will do quite well. But I must ask about this bond. How does that happen? That the connection exists, I know, since I felt the pull of it in my own blood. But I have wondered even as I experienced it. Does everyone you feed on develop a bond with you?"

"Yes. And no. The bond is there, certainly, but one must exploit it, and that is something I ordinarily do not do. Unless there is a need. And tonight we have the need. Let us go and claim our guard, our brave and daring captain who likes nothing better than kisses from strange ladies."

We were fortunate in that he was on duty again this evening. Once again he emerged out of the shadows and began to explain to us the workings of the device. But when I moved closer to him and looked him dead in the eye, he stopped in midsentence and stared.

"Yes," I said, walking up to him and running my hand down his arm. "I have returned for you, *mon Capitaine.*" I stretched up on my toes and kissed him full on the lips, still maintaining eye contact.

"But, but," he stammered a bit, "that was only a dream. Wasn't it?"

I laughed. "Perhaps it was a dream. And perhaps it was not. But for now, I wish you to remember me again."

His eyes widened and his hand went to his neck. "I remember your kisses, lady. Do you want more? Everything I have is at your disposal."

"What is your name?"

"Raoul Mountaigne."

"Ah, a nice strong name for a nice strong man. Do you like the service you give here, Raoul?"

He glanced around. "The nights get lonely and cold sometimes. And I have been having the strangest feelings, even"—and he gave a wan smile—"before that dream of you. As I stand and watch I think I see the souls of those who have died here rising up out of the ground. And while I know in my head that it is only fog and mist, my heart thinks differently."

"And so you do not like your post?"

"In short, no. But a duty is a duty and I have been assigned this one." He inclined his head toward the guillotine. "I would not dare to leave it. Watching this device at work has a not so strange way of warning one off the thoughts of shirking."

I laughed and after a second he joined me. "No doubt, Raoul. And your sense of duty is to be greatly admired. But if you had another alternative? Serving two beautiful ladies perhaps? With an opportunity to travel and see the wonders of the world?"

He laughed. "If I left my post, I'd need to travel and travel quickly. And yet, it is tempting. Especially if I am to assume that the two beautiful ladies are standing in front of me."

I nodded. "What time do you get off duty, Raoul?"

"Midnight, Mademoiselle."

"Good. Come to the House of the Swan no later than half past twelve and ask for Mademoiselle Courbet. You know where the house is?"

"Most certainly."

I took his face between my hands and pulled it down to me, so that I could kiss him again. "Do not fail me, Raoul, and you will be well rewarded."

He bowed. "I will be there, Mademoiselle."

Monique pulled me aside and whispered in my ear, "Is that all there is to it?"

Nodding, I linked my arm into hers and began to lead her away. "For the moment, yes. But he is only intrigued now. Later we will make sure that he is enraptured."

"And so now I can feed?"

"Yes, of course, my little lamb, er, tiger." I gave an amused snort. "It will take some getting used to you as a tiger. Now, do you want an easy conquest? Or do you want a full-fledged hunt?"

She thought for a minute. "I am tempted to want the hunt and yet perhaps it would be best the first time to take the easy way."

"Fine, *mon chou,* it is your choice, there is no difference between the two so far as your stomach is concerned."

Once we returned to the house, I made my way up the stairs but told her to go to the main room, choose her victim, and bring him back to me. I changed from my outdoor dress to a pink silk dressing gown, brushed my hair in front of the mirror, then began to pull the cork on a bottle of wine, setting out three glasses.

The knock on the door coming as soon as it did surprised me; It would have taken a much longer time had it been I doing the choosing. But she was hungry and inexperienced and had, I saw when they entered the room, picked a man who closely resembled Eduard. As I thought about it, though, I realized that I was not particularly surprised by this, her choice, considering the mixed feelings she had expressed about Eduard. I myself had chosen for my first victim a man who could have been my father—in appearance, in age, and in social standing.

Max had not been surprised either, when I told him why I had selected that one out of the many I could have chosen. "It is the way it is, at first. We look for someone familiar, someone who makes us angry and yet comfortable at the same time." In his always infuriating manner, he had refused to tell me who his first victim resembled. "Bastard."

"Mademoiselle?" Monique's young man seemed confused by the word and I laughed.

"Not you, good Monsieur, I assure you. Please come in and make yourself comfortable."

As I poured the three glasses of wine, I realized with a touch of laughter that this situation was much like my first evening with Max and Victor. I wondered if this young man would faint dead away in front of the fire as I did. But no, I was not like Max or Victor—their main goals always seemed to be intimidation and fear. My only wish was to be left alone so that I could feed in safety. And if there was a little bit of fun to be had in the bargain, so much the better.

Letting Monique take the lead, I sat down in front of the hearth and stared at the fire, watching it dance and twist, imagining that I saw a face in the flames. Like Raoul I could see the ghosts and still would not believe. Strange, given the sort of creature that I was, that I was so skeptical. But, if you had asked up until the moment I'd met Max, I'd have said that the existence of vampires was nothing more than a myth.

Perhaps then I would believe in ghosts only when I was one. Laughing, I picked up a small chip of wood that had fallen from the basket and tossed it onto the fire, thinking *If I must be dead to believe, I can easily do without belief.*

Monique cleared her throat and I turned my attention back to the situation at hand; she'd managed to peel back the young man's shirt collar and jabot, but had stopped there, unsure of how to proceed. She shot me a pleading look and

I got up from the hearth and went over to them where they sat together on the lounge.

"And what is your name, young man?"

"Jean-Paul."

"Well then, Jean-Paul, tell me something. Have you ever had a woman?"

He smiled. "But of course, Mademoiselle. Many women."

"Ah." Reaching down and taking his hand, I brought it to my mouth and licked his fingers. "And have you ever had two women? At one time?"

His eyes darted back and forth between us and his breathing grew noticeably heavier. "No, not exactly, Mademoiselle, but I am sure I can oblige if that is what you want."

I smiled. "It is indeed what we want. Come to the bed, Jean, and we will show you how one strong man can satisfy the appetites of two hungry ladies."

Monique giggled and followed us, joined me in laying him down and stripping him naked, then stripping ourselves and settling in one on either side of him. That he was intrigued by the situation was obvious and Monique gave a low whistle of appreciation. "Very impressive, Jean, certainly there is enough of you for both of us."

"I would hope so." Proud of his manhood and intoxicated with our attentions, Jean put his arms around us and pulled us both in close, so that each of our heads rested on his shoulders. I glanced over his chest at Monique and gave a slight nod.

She smiled back at me and I saw that her fangs

had lengthened, but she seemed uncertain about their placement. I nodded to her again.

"Close your eyes, Jean." I brushed my hand over his face, "And keep them closed. We have a little surprise for you. You do like surprises, do you not?"

He laughed. "Surprises from two such as you are always welcome."

I gave him a playful little slap across the cheek. "Then close your eyes or there will be no surprise."

"Yes, Mademoiselle," he said meekly and obeyed.

I opened my mouth wider than I would ordinarily have, curling my upper lip back and pulling my lower jaw in, exaggerating the position and the motion so that Monique could see and learn.

She did the same and when I nodded, she lowered her mouth to his neck.

It was a clumsy bite, of course, being her first. And it must have been painful; his eyes flew open in panic and he jumped, trying to push her away. Quickly, I moved over top of him and impaled myself on him, rising and falling slowly at first and then with more urgency, until he closed his eyes again and moaned in pleasure.

After he reached his orgasm, I motioned for her to take her mouth away. She peered up at me, gave a low growl, but withdrew her fangs. At the same time, I slid myself off of Jean.

And it was over. She licked her lips and gave me a triumphant smile. I snuggled up next to a tired Jean. "Sleep for a while, *mon cher,*" I told him, "and when you awaken you will remember none of what happened here. Do you understand?"

He nodded and mumbled his assent.

"Good. Now sleep."

We dressed him again and woke him up, sending him on his way a tired but sated man. Although he would have no remembrance of how he came to be that way, still he would look back on this night and smile without knowing why.

"Always give something back, Monique," I said after he walked out the door. "Never steal what you must take; let them think they are giving it freely and they will forget more easily."

"So how did the tiger cub do, Maman?"

I leaned over and kissed her on the lips, flicking my tongue inside her mouth for a taste of Jean's blood. "You did well, Monique. He was young and strong and eager. You did not take too much and you did not take too little. And you did not choke or cough; often the first taste is bitter and sour."

"It did not taste bitter or sour to me, Vivienne. It was as sweet and as thick as honey." She smiled. "When can I do it again?"

Twenty

It proved to be as busy a night as the previous was, and although the tasks involved were more pleasant, they were no less grueling. No sooner had we sent Jean-Paul on his way than Raoul appeared as ordered.

As she had with Jean-Paul, Monique escorted Raoul to our room, gave him a glass of wine, and encouraged him to get comfortable. This time, though, it was I who sat on the lounge with him while Monique watched.

Holding his hands and looking into his eyes, I spoke to him for a while, explaining the tasks expected of him. As duties went, none of them were particularly onerous, but I wanted to make sure that he understood completely what it was he needed to learn to do.

After he was questioned and found correct on all counts we moved on.

"What do you think I am, Raoul?"

He shrugged. "To be honest, Mademoiselle, I am not sure. It would seem that you are one of the old myths come to life, if such a thing in our enlightened age is possible. My mother's mother would tell stories of the dead or the undead rising from their graves to suck the life from the living. But I always assumed they were stories told to frighten the children. And I always assumed they were like dead creatures, bloated and ugly and incapable of human speech, not beautiful and full of life like you."

I smiled. "Thank you, Raoul."

"If you had wings, I would think you an angel. Not one of the undead."

I laughed, the high-pitched peals echoing off the walls. "If I am an angel, *mon Capitaine,* then I am one of the fallen. But for that matter, I do have wings. I shall show you." I slipped out of my dressing gown and stood naked in front of him. "Watch."

I closed my eyes for a second, gathering my thoughts and my strength. Then I folded my arms around me and dropped to a crouch. I shifted awareness of my humanlike form into another familiar one. Shadows grew up from the floor and began to engulf my body, spreading darkness over every available bit of skin. Feathers began to emerge from the shadows, feathers soft yet piercing, covering me completely. I stretched my neck up and felt it grow, felt my face shrink back in on itself and my nose grow into a long graceful beak. Within seconds the transformation was complete and I was now a giant black swan. Monique gave a small gasp as I spread my wings wide. She had not known this was possible. And Raoul was entranced.

In an instant, I banished the feathers and my skin grew tawny and furred. The wings disappeared, my neck shrank, and my body elongated, growing sturdy and well muscled. I felt vicious claws emerge from what had been my hands and feet and were now the deadly paws of an African lioness. Putting my head back, I gave a loud roar. Monique laughed in delight and Raoul flinched.

In another instant, I banished the fur and the claws, along with all the other attributes of a physical body. For one short moment, I was no longer perceivable by the human eye and both of them looked around the room in dismay. Quickly I pulled to me the mists of the night, curled the wisps around to approximate the size and shape of my human form. And then with one great effort of thought, I was back in my human form, standing naked in front of them.

"And that, Raoul," I said, putting on my dressing gown once more, "that is the sort of creature you have been called to serve. Will you stay?"

If he refused, I would have to kill him here and now. That was ever the risk one took when revealing the truth. Fortunately, he smiled shyly and dropped to his knees in front of me. "Gladly, lady. I would give you my life if you asked."

"Good. I hope that giving of your life will never be necessary. Now get up off the floor, Raoul, and let me seal this deal with a kiss."

He came to me and I enfolded him in the pink silk sleeves of my gown. Then I bent him over my arm as if in a dance and drank from him, just a token swallow or two. His blood tasted fresh and clean and I sighed softly as I released him from my grasp.

"One more thing, Raoul, and you will be free to go and arrange that which you need to arrange to make it possible for you to serve us."

"Whatever you ask, Mademoiselle."

"First, you are to call me Vivienne. I do not care for the formality of titles. And second." I went to my dressing table and opened up a jewel box, finding an ornate cloak pin. I pricked my finger with the tip and walked over to him. "Open your mouth."

He did so, putting his head back and his tongue out, a gesture most often seen at church. But this was no holy communion, it was not the blood of Christ, it was my blood. I squeezed my finger over his opened mouth, forcing three drops of that precious fluid to fall upon his tongue. More than that and he might, over time, transform into a vampire. And I wished him to remain human and under my control.

He swallowed and choked. The taste was bitter no doubt, but after his initial reaction, his face softened into a smile and his skin seemed to glow. I kissed his cheek and smiled back at him.

"Now go, Raoul, and make your arrangements. I wish you to be back here an hour before dawn and I will tell you then your tasks for the day."

"Until then, Vivienne," and he bowed and left the room.

"Do you think he'll be back?" Monique spoke from the corner of the room where she'd observed the ritual.

"He could not stay away now for any reason in the world; he would desert the deathbed of his mother to come to me. A good choice, Monique, he will serve us quite well. Tomorrow we will have him make all the necessary arrangements for us to leave Paris."

She gave a short little surprised squeak. "We're leaving Paris? Why?"

"Why not? Eduard is gone. Running the House of the Swan has become wearisome, especially now. Some of the women have approached me about taking over the ownership and management of the business; I believe they have earned that chance. Plus, I have become just a bit too visible, too accessible here to all too many people. I wish to travel in secrecy for a while."

"But," she stammered, "but I had no idea. I do not wish to leave Paris."

"I have been thinking about this for a while now, Monique. Long before you showed up on my doorstep. I have purchased a small chateau in the mountains; I assure you it is at least as plush as this house, perhaps more so. And there is a good-sized village nearby so that we will not suffer for lack of food. What is there for us here that we cannot have in greater safety elsewhere?"

I walked over to her and gave her a hug. "I know, change is frightening and you have lived your whole life in this one city. But the world is a wonderful place and it is time to move on. I have had more than enough of this revolution and wish to be as far away as possible. And perhaps in another place, the memories of the recent events will be less painful."

What I did not voice to her was that my chateau had been acquired in secrecy. Neither Max nor Victor knew that it existed and I would not have to fear her death at their hands. Their promises not to interfere meant nothing, I knew. And Max already had taken a dislike to Monique much as he had to Diego.

"I see," she said, "you miss Eduard and wish to be away from all of it. And of course, you are right. It will be an exciting adventure for us. I just had never considered the possibility; I was born here in Paris and I thought I would live out my life here and then die. But now." She clapped her hands together like a child receiving a gift. "Now the entire world is open to me. And it is frightening and exhilarating at the same time."

"Exactly as life should be."

She smiled then and all was well.

I kept Raoul quite busy over the next few days. His first order of business was to acquire Monique her own coffin. I found that I could not sleep when she was with me, so unaccustomed was I to having another of my kind present. After that, she and I busied ourselves with packing and he acquired a team of horses and a large enough coach to accommodate both our coffins and our personal articles.

Cecile and some of the other women took over the management of the house. My absence would make no difference; we had acquired a good reputation over the years, if such a thing is at all possible for a brothel. Men knew that the House was fair and clean and relatively sedate and discreet. The customers would continue to come and I needn't fear that my desire for escape would affect anyone else.

Monique alternated between bouts of pouting and rushes of excitement about our departure. She showed great agility, though, in learning the life of the vampire quickly and well. Her hunts were extremely successful. She could subdue the largest man with just a touch and a glance; the amount of blood she drew was never too much or too little, and her victims always forgot.

"And for tonight, Vivienne," she said on our last night in Paris, "I would like to hunt alone. I feel that I am ready and that this is something that will further my learning."

I was delighted. "Yes, *ma chere*, that is a wonderful idea. Just do not miss the time."

She laughed and gave me a hug and a kiss on the cheek. "Yes, Maman, I will be back home before dawn. Thank you."

"For what?"

"Everything," she said, waving as she went out the door. "Everything and nothing."

I watched from the window until she moved out of my sight. "Hunt well, my little lamb. Walk softly and safely this night until you come back to me."

But dawn came without Monique. I should have suspected that she would run away from me; that her love for the city of her birth was greater than her love for me. But I had not realized how strong the ties had been. I didn't fear that she was dead; the bonds between us would let me know if that had occurred. There existed still that little nagging presence of her, even after Raoul gave up the daytime search and I abandoned the night one.

Finally I grew angry at her ungrateful desertion and yelled out the window. "The city is now yours, you little bitch, and I hope it treats you as you deserve." A childish gesture, I knew, but I was hurt. She could at least have said good-bye.

As I climbed into my coffin I looked over at Raoul, drowsing by the fire. "Make the necessary preparations, *mon Capitaine,* we leave tomorrow."

It is always amazing to me how quickly the time passes. For one such as I the years seem to run together. I'd had so many lovers, so many servants, so many victims, and all of their faces blend into one in my mind. It is almost as if there is no time; every moment is the same moment, every taste of blood is the same taste.

In the two centuries that followed my self-imposed exile from Paris, I did not attempt to transform a vampire companion for myself. Nor did I attempt to contact any of the others of my kind. The experience with Diego and Max was too saddening and the desertion of Monique too much of a betrayal for me to have the heart and desire to go forward. I had once again become incapable of love.

So I lived as a solitary creature, a vampire alone, seeking out humans only for food and for satisfaction of my sexual desire. At first I had employed a series of protecting servants. Raoul served me loyally for many years, his human system fortified and the ravages of time slowed for him by small doses of my blood. But even he grew old and died, and subsequent protectors lived even fewer years, until eventually the apathy and disbelief of human beings made their positions unnecessary and I found I could survive quite well without them.

And the years fell around me, like blossoms shaken off a tree in the wind. I watched the world change around me while I, alone and unknown, remained unchanged. The demon in the mirror smiled and lied and continued without end, without a companion and without love.

And that is the way I thought I always wanted it to be.

Part Two

Twenty-one

New York City: Cadre headquarters, present day

"Je t'emmerde, espece de porc a la manque!" I hung up the phone, and swept the entire contents of the damned desk on the floor.

Monique, now my personal assistant, came into the office at my outburst, looking over at me with a tolerant smile on her face. She had grown used to my tirades. "So, who is the worthless pig you were talking to this time?"

"Does it matter?" I stood up and paced around the room, flinging my arms up in the air in frustration. "This having to deal with humans all the time is making me crazy. Had I known this job entailed diplomacy I would have turned it down."

"As I remember, Vivienne . . ." She began to pick up the items from the carpet and set them back on the desk surface. "You really had no choice."

Ignoring her response, I continued my ranting. "Humans! It is all well and good when one chooses to seek them out for food. Or even sex, for that matter. But now? Now I must flatter this one. And threaten another. Keep the balance and keep the peace." I shook my head. "And is that not enough for one vampire to handle?"

From the corner of the room where she was crawling on hands and knees gathering paper clips, Monique gave an absent response. "Is it?"

"No, but of course it is not enough. Now all the Cadre members with more than a hundred years under their belts are petitioning to become house leaders. I ask you, Monique, how many leaders can we possibly need? And then there are all these requests to install new vampires. How long will it be before this whole damned city is filled with nothing but bloodsuckers? Where will we all be then?"

Monique stood up from the floor, paper clips clutched in her fists. She dropped them into a crystal bowl that miraculously had escaped breaking. Then, with a twisted smile, she repositioned the telephone and picked up the receiver, putting it to her ear for a second, holding it out to me with a nod. "Not broken yet, *mon chou*, perhaps you'd like to try again."

"No. It won't help." I flopped back down into my chair, like a petulant child, resting my elbows on the desk and my chin in my hands. "They'll just bring in a new one."

She came up behind me and wrapped her arms around my neck, placing a kiss on the top of my head. "My dear Vivienne, I can't believe you are taking this so seriously. It's not like you."

I reached up and ran my fingers over the top of her short black hair. "I can scarcely believe it myself. Perhaps I will outgrow it."

She laughed softly and walked over to the door, checking the clock on the wall. "If you don't need anything else, Vivienne, I'd like to go now. I want to get out before all the good ones are taken."

"Hunting tonight?"

"Yes." Her voice dropped to a husky whisper. "Come with me. It would be fun—just like the good old days."

I met her eyes, saw the weight of her years, and for just a second I wondered who she was and why she was here. Ten years ago she had reappeared in my life abruptly and without warning or explanation. And I had taken her back into my world with no recriminations or accusations; *truly,* I rationalized, *all she had done to me was run away, not much harm in that.* I had wished to leave Paris and she had wished to stay. Such a very small betrayal in the overall scheme of things.

And yet, those years spent apart were hidden from me and she did not speak of them. *Fair enough,* I thought, *we all have our own personal demons of which we do not talk.* She was still Monique and I loved her, in my way, remembering the poor little lost lamb she had been. But her eyes were those of a stranger, until they filled with flames of lust and hunger. And at times like that I knew her, knew that the bond of her making still held us together. Her eyes were like my own and what they offered me was so very tempting. We had spent countless nights together after her return, hunting and feeding and making love to so many in so many different ways. And the games she devised were intriguing and amusing.

I sighed. Although I was hungry, I had no time for the games. "No." I shook my head reluctantly and sighed again. "I'm expecting more phone calls."

"Suit yourself." She leaned over the desk and kissed me lightly on the cheek. "Maybe some other night."

"Monique?"

She stopped in the doorway and turned to me expectantly. "Yes, *mon amie?*"

"Turn the lights out when you leave."

I do not know how long I sat there behind my desk in the darkness. Vampires do not measure time as humans do. A second, a decade, a century—all seemed much the same to those who have an endless span of years. I preferred not to think of it most of the time, having known perfectly sane creatures who drove themselves to madness with the contemplation of eternity. I enjoyed my life too much to want to spend it insane. And why should I not enjoy my life? What else could there be for one such as I? Love was a nightmare, an emotion best kept under lock and key. As a being incapable of love, I had no spouse, no child, nothing to burden me in the way my one and only blood sister was burdened. The only responsibility I carried was my position as leader of the Cadre, a dubious distinction at best. What did it matter the sort of leadership this clan of ancient vampires received? We knew we were the superior beings; humankind had no knowledge of us and therefore had no fear. Without fear there can be no hate and without hate, no violence capable of threatening our existence. Safe and secure, locked away in our underground warren, we were guarded by the disbelief of the rest of the world. Our anonymity kept us alive; even as we moved among them, fed upon them, interacted with them, we remained invisible. All in all, not a bad deal. Life was good.

Except that I was trapped here taking care of Cadre business. I sat for a while longer, tapping my long, white-lacquered nails on the desk in boredom, glaring at the phone, daring it to ring, hoping it would not.

Finally, I jumped up. "Monique is right, I shouldn't care about any of this. And so"—I reached over and turned on the answering machine—"I am now finished."

I wound my way through the empty hallways, pushed the button for the elevator when I reached it. When Victor was still in town and still in charge, it seemed that this place was a hotbed of activity. But now it was dead. *As dead as its inhabitants,* I thought and gave a low laugh. Deader, actually, since the inhabitants here had at least a semblance of life. I heard the phone ring in my office, echoing once off the walls, followed by the phone greeting, short and sweet: "Name, number, message. At the beep," then Monique's throaty laugh and the actual beep of the machine. There was a pause, a cough, and another pause, until a faint, almost familiar voice said, "Monique? Vivienne?"

"Forget it, Monsieur, whoever the hell you are," I said as the elevator door opened and I got on, giggling, "we have all gone fishing." The doors closed and I noticed someone had left the key in the lock that opened the panel allowing one access to the business quarters and the sleeping quarters. I used the key, so I wouldn't have to rummage around in my bag for mine, and pushed the button for my floor. Then I closed the panel and locked it, taking the key with me, making a mental note to issue a warning on Monday. People around here were getting sloppy and complacent.

I understood that tendency. In fact, I was guilty of it more than once, even during the most recent crisis that had left several of our members dead, a crisis now that most of the Cadre referred to as the Martin fiasco. Fortunately I had not been in charge then—Victor had abdicated his rule in favor of Mitchell Greer, the husband of my sister. Mitch had governed well, much better than I ever had or would. *If only,* I thought for probably the hundredth time, *if only he would take it again.* I gave a low laugh; that was a vain hope. He would do it but only if *she* asked, and of course she would not. And I couldn't blame her for that; if he were mine, I'd guard him too. So I was back to it again; the governing of the Cadre rested in my hands.

But not now, I reminded myself as I opened the door to my room. "Even the queen gets a day off now and then." I winked at my image in the large wardrobe mirror.

I put on a pair of faded jeans, skintight and torn in the appropriate places. Topped off with a cropped pink mohair sweater, I looked even younger than normal. I accentuated this youthful appearance by putting my hair into two pigtails at the top of my head, elastic bands with little pink beads holding them in place. Looking in the mirror, I bobbed my head to make sure the hair had the appropriate bounce, checked out the back of my jeans to admire the curve of my ass and the small bits of white flesh shining through.

"Cool," I said, practicing the dialect I would

need to speak, and with a giggle I shook my head, as if in time to some music. "Man, this band is unfuckingbelievable!" Although most of the places I hunted were too noisy for my voice to be heard, still I prided myself on the ability to blend. My normal accent would be too distinctive and I did not like leaving clues behind me. If something went wrong, if fragments of memories remained with my victim, I did not want trouble following me back. Vivienne's first rule—protect the place you sleep.

The place at which I slept was Cadre headquarters, located levels below one of the city's most upscale restaurants. The Imperial had existed in one form or another for almost as long as I remembered. Victor Leupold Lange owned it, but he was currently away in New Orleans playing house with the daughter of my sister. An odd relationship; he being the oldest of us and she just newly transformed. But since my personal war had always been waged against Max and Max alone, I couldn't begrudge Victor what little bit of comfort he had found with the girl. And she, at least, would get the training her mother had not received. Victor had turned over the management of the restaurant and the Cadre several years prior. In fact, he had abdicated his positions so abruptly and had withdrawn from life so completely that many of us feared he would commit suicide. The girl, Lily, saved his life. It was my fondest hope that someday he would want control of this organization again and I would be free.

I caught the elevator up from my room and moved down the hallway toward the employee entrance. One of the largest men I had ever encountered stood there, guarding one of the few ways into the place. I had met him about a year ago, playing piano in a blues club in New Orleans. He had been a great find and proved to be quite loyal to his maker. I smiled at him as I passed. "Claude, how are you this evening?"

"Well, Miss Courbet. And if I may say so, you're looking fantastic as usual."

"Thank you, Claude. If anyone is looking for me, I'll be out for a bit. Or a bite."

He gave a small laugh. "It's a fine evening for a hunt."

"*Oui,* but then when isn't it? Has Monique left?"

"Some time ago."

"Ah." I stood looking up at him for a second. He really was huge. Then I patted him on the arm. "I suppose I will be going then. Good night."

"Good night and good hunting, Miss Courbet."

Twenty-two

Once on the street I walked for several blocks before hailing a cab to take me to the place I chose for this evening, an under-twenty-one dance club. Sweeter meat than my normal fare, I thought with a giggle as I paid the cab driver and got out to stand in line with the rest of the young people, observing their interactions and eventually, before gaining access, making the acquaintance of another girl who had come by herself.

Her name was Heather, her hair was purple, and she was dressed all in black.

"Vivvi," I said with a calculatedly shy smile. "Have you been here before?"

"Vinnie?" she asked, or rather yelled, since we were standing right outside the open door and the band had already started.

"No, Vivvi. Lots of *V*s. It looks cool when I sign my name."

Heather laughed. "Yeah, I guess it would. My name is so ordinary, it's like everyone is called Heather these days. I want to change it, but my mom freaks whenever I mention it."

"Yeah." I rolled my eyes and nodded my head

in appreciation of the vileness of some parents. "My dad's like that too. What an asshole he is. I mean you just want to say, 'Go away and leave me alone,' you know?"

Heather laughed and I knew we had bonded. A little early in the evening, perhaps, but I'd found my target. It was always easy to find suitable prey; so many lonely, desperate people in this city, anxious to make contact, to reach out to someone else, seeking comfort, seeking approval, seeking love. This girl was no different, but she was strong and healthy and would hardly miss what I would take. Some vampires only preyed on the same type of person over and over again. I craved variety and even if I did not, blood was blood, male, female, young or old: each served their purpose admirably. And I saw no need to leave a discernable pattern.

"Nothing to trace," I said.

"What?"

We had moved into the main room of the club by now. The band was deafening and the sea of bodies intoxicating. I didn't need liquor to get my high. "Nothing," I screamed back at her. "Wanna dance?"

An older woman would have taken offense at the suggestion, but Heather was young enough so that dancing with other women, provided it wasn't slow dancing, was perfectly acceptable.

We joined the other dancers on the floor, what seemed like hundreds of human bodies crowded together, with their scent of blood and sweat and the perfume of arousal. The entire experience was so intense that it hurt, generating a physical craving and longing that made me ache deep inside. Oh, how I longed to drink them all, to hold them all tightly in my arms, to capture their sweet essences and keep them with me forever.

But I could not have them all. Instead I intensified my efforts with the one I had chosen and smiled at Heather. She smiled back, lost in the dancing almost as much as I was lost in the flood of sensations. Her small breasts jiggled against her black T-shirt, circles of perspiration grew under her arms, and still we danced, until she was breathless and laughing.

I leaned over to her after three or four numbers by the band. "I need to go to the girls' room. You want to come?"

"Might as well," she shouted back, "it'll be less crowded now than when the band takes a break."

The line for the ladies' room stretched almost to the dance floor, and I laughed. "If this is less crowded, I don't think I want to see it any other time."

"Yeah," Heather agreed, "do you need to go really bad?"

"Yes, I do. Think they'll let me cut ahead?"

Heather shook her head. "This crowd? No way. But you know, I know another place, just down the street. Small little neighborhood type bar, we could go there, it's not usually too crowded and"—she gave me a sly look—"the bartender likes me. He'll give us something a little stronger to drink than soda if we ask him nice."

"Sounds good to me." I wrapped an arm around her waist and we left the club, trying to keep in step with each other, giggling as we walked the two blocks to the bar she spoke of.

Charlie's Place was perfect. Dark and seedy, with

a clientele interested only in getting drunker. Two obviously underage girls arriving made little impact on their plans. After gesturing me into a back booth, Heather stopped off at the bar and got us both a beer. Then she slid into the seat next to me so that both of us were facing away from the bar and slid one of the mugs in my direction.

"If I sit looking at him," she whispered to me, her breath tickling the hairs on my neck, "it gives me the creeps. He's a nice guy, yeah, but he's so old."

"Yeah." Old? The bartender was a child, probably no more than twenty-eight or -nine. I turned my head to look at him again and she nudged my arm.

"Oh, no, don't look. Don't encourage him, he'll come over if you show too much interest."

Still, as he kept the beer flowing, she softened toward him. Not quite the effect I was hoping for. I needed to get her alone, not to get her all dewy-eyed over him. No doubt I could persuade her, but I preferred it when they came with me of their own free will; it didn't seem sporting the other way. And yet, I was very hungry.

"He's not all that bad," she was saying, "he's sort of cute, really. Just older enough to make it feel weird, you know?"

I looked into her eyes and laid my hand on her arm. Her skin was so warm, so vibrant. "You can do better than him," I said.

"Do you think so?" Her eyes widened, but she didn't pull away from me.

"Oh, definitely." My voice sounded lower, expectant. "You're beautiful, Heather. I can't believe you don't know that."

I kept my eyes on her; she blushed, then smiled. "Think so?" She repeated the question.

I nodded. "Of course. I would never lie to you, *mon amie.*" Then I giggled, trying to drop back into my role. "Anyway, I really need to pee right now. Where is the bathroom?"

She slid over and got up from the bench, swaying just a bit. "I'll show you, I need to go too."

I was glad to see that it was a bathroom with several stalls, even gladder that it was completely empty. Heather rushed into one of the stalls and I took the one next to her, not needing it, of course, but pretending. She talked to me the whole time and when her flow stopped, I rustled the paper a bit, flushed my toilet, and went to the sink, taking the elastic bands out of my hair and combing through it with my fingers.

I heard the rasping sound of the zipper of her jeans. Her door flew open and she came out with a giggle. "Man, I really needed to go." She washed her hands, and stood at the mirror next to me. The dim light of the bathroom made her hair look almost black and I realized why I'd felt so drawn to her. She reminded me of Monique when I had first met her. Poor little waif.

I reached over and pulled back Heather's hair, fastening it with one of the bands I'd taken out of my own hair. "See?" I said, standing behind her and whispering in her ear while maintaining eye contact in the mirror. "Your face has classical lines, your cheekbones are exquisite, and your eyes? They are magnificent. You are a beauty."

It really wasn't fair, I didn't have to play with her this way. She would have done anything that I asked of her at any time, but I needed this contact, the reassurance that, despite being a monster underneath, I could be and still was desirable. It wasn't really sex I was looking for; instead I wanted a willing surrender.

She turned around and reached a trembling hand out to touch my face. Her eyes were distant and glazed over. A willing surrender? I laughed inwardly at my conceit. *Not this time, Vivienne,* I thought, *this girl is not Monique.* But still I hungered for her. Without saying another word, I pulled her to me and fastened my mouth to her neck.

The taste of her was worth all of the time I had spent seducing her. Each sip brought her closer to me; as I drank her blood, I also absorbed some of her spirit, her youth, her beauty. And in a hundred years when she would be dead, I would still hold a part of her, a feel of the girl she was this evening, a photograph etched in memory.

She moaned in my arms and I took my mouth away, licking the small puncture wounds there. Then I pulled her hair free of the elastic and brushed it down over her neck. "Such a sweet girl," I whispered to her. "You will not remember this, you will not remember me for what I am. I am just a girl you met, not important, easily forgettable. But I will carry you with me forever."

I kissed her on the lips then and left her standing in the bathroom, swaying slightly and holding on to the sink. Her bartender friend would make sure that she got home.

I slowly made my way back to Cadre headquarters, avoiding further contact with humans, wanting to hold her sweetness in my mouth as long as I could.

I have heard that some of my kind do not sleep in coffins, there being no scientific necessity for such an arrangement. I have been told that a simple bed can suffice; as long as the room was not accessible to sunlight one would be completely safe. That may be true in modern days, and I have at times slept so, but my instincts have always called out for the safety of an enclosed area. My own particular coffin had been custom made; lined with steel plates, equipped with three heavy bolts for added protection, and fitted with a pink satin-covered mattress and pillows. Ostentatious, perhaps, and possibly unnecessary, but it was comfortable and secure.

Shortly before dawn then, I changed into a white silk nightgown and crawled into my haven, pulling the inner locks shut, settling into the pillows, anticipating with delight the day's sleep, the sweet dreamless void. I smiled; it had been a good hunt.

Twenty-three

The next evening fell, much like the previous evening and the one before that. Once again I was trapped in my office in Cadre headquarters, deep within the bowels of the Imperial. But at least I had only a short amount of time to spend here, since tonight was the Masquerade at Dangerous Crossings. I chuckled to myself about the club. I'd purchased it from Deirdre who'd inherited it from Max in the days it had been called the Ballroom of Romance.

I'd had no patience for romance for many many years and so immediately after acquiring the place, I gutted it and converted into a borderline S&M club. It had turned out to be a huge success. People would wait in line for hours to gain admittance and many would pay a fairly exorbitant amount of money for the privilege of hanging in my dungeon rooms, in the hopes that I might choose one of them and feed. Perhaps it seemed foolhardy to expose my nature so blatantly, but no one believed that I could be a true vampire.

And so Dangerous Crossing was born and opened to rave reviews from the magazine critics. It all came as no surprise to me. If my years had taught me anything, it was that the human heart had the capacity to seek out and embrace pain with uncanny accuracy.

And not just the human heart. The planned masquerade brought memories of other times. Of how Eduard and I had danced and laughed and made love. That it was love, I had no doubt. Never before and never since had I experienced the emotion. And although I knew him for only a short amount of time, and lost him, I could close my eyes and catch the scent of him in the air, the touch of him on my skin. I allowed my thoughts to form into fantasies of Paris and a time that never existed, one during which Eduard was not executed. We would walk the nighttime streets arm in arm and in silence, the fullness of our hearts needing no words. We would stroll past the Place du Carroussel and see nothing more threatening than our own shadows on the sides of the buildings, hear nothing more horrible than the steady patter of rain on the roofs and the cobblestones. Here the guillotine never existed and citizens of France did not kill their own. And I would laugh and tell him the story of the dream I had, of the revolution and how he had been killed. "But I am not dead," he would say, "I am here, with you. And will always be."

When the phone rang again, I jumped, having lost myself chasing ghosts down the rain-drenched streets of Paris's yesterdays. I glared at the phone wondering which city government buffoon was calling, wondering what petty problem would soon become the Cadre's problem and, by extension, mine. I even played with the idea of not answering. But with the sixth ring I picked it up, making a silent note to set the answering machine when this call was over.

"Yes?"

"Vivienne?" The voice was low-pitched and distant.

"Yes?"

"Vivienne Courbet?"

"Yes. That is I. What is it you want?"

There was a pause on the other end of the line, followed by a deep exhalation of breath that might have been a sigh. "This is a private line, Monsieur." I gave a small laugh. "And I am not one to entertain anonymous obscenities. State your business and your name. Or I will hang up."

"No, you misunderstand." The caller sighed again. "Do not hang up. I have a message for you."

"Well?"

"Prenez garde à la fuite du temps."

The line went dead and as I set the receiver down, I noticed that my hand was shaking. Beware the passage of time, he had said.

It was not a good message. And I had too many years behind me of which to beware. A chill shivered up my spine. Then I stood up and hugged my arms to myself. "Foo, it is stupid to be frightened. They are only words. And"—I reached over and turned on the desk lamp, foolishly searching the corners of the room for the shadows of yesterdays—"words cannot hurt me."

"I should hope not, Vivienne." The deep voice was shaded with laughter and I jumped, startled, then looked up to see the smiling face of Dr. John Samuels. "But you do know that it's not healthy to be talking to yourself, don't you?"

"Sam, *mon cher,* do not attempt to analyze me. You are not my psychiatrist. And do not tease me. I have had a bad day and an even worse night."

He walked across the room and deposited a light kiss on my cheek, correctly gauging my mood and sensing that I wished no prolonged demonstrations. I sighed. *Ah, Sam,* I thought, *how can you be so right for me and yet so wrong all at the same time?* I knew better than to get involved in a serious relationship with a human. Over three hundred years of experience taught me that it just wouldn't work. And yet, here I was again, walking the tightrope, balancing needs and emotions, hoping to forestall or avoid the fall. I sighed again and shook my head slightly, forcing my face into a brilliant grin and stretching up on my toes to give him a kiss back.

"So, how was your day? Did you manage to get Mitch and Deirdre on the phone? Did you get them to come to my party?"

"No such luck," Sam said. "Deirdre was determined that they stay where they are for now, to spend some time alone. And they both sounded like they were enjoying living in England again." He shrugged and then smiled. "I don't believe I ever met a more stubborn couple. It's a bit of a miracle to even have them back together again. She was so adamant after he left and he was so guilt-ridden that he had been tricked into leaving."

I laughed. "If you ask me, Sam my sweet, the two of them need to relax; all that thinking and questioning can make one crazy. They should let it all go, learn how to have fun, and just exist."

"In short, they should become more like you?"

"Exactly, *mon cher.* For am I not the perfect being?"

Sam did not laugh as I meant him to. Instead he shook his head and gave me a questioning look. "A perfect being should not be frightened when a friend appears in her doorway. Don't try to fool me, Vivienne, what's wrong?"

"Nothing is wrong," I began to insist, but the phone rang and I reacted with a small sudden intake of breath.

"Nothing? Is it nothing that you can be frightened at the sound of the phone ringing?"

I glared at him, then glared at the phone as it continued to ring. I reached my hand out to pick it up, but pulled it back to my side when I saw that it was shaking.

"I am not going to answer that. I've had enough of business to last me an eternity. Therefore, I declare this workday over." As if to punctuate my words, the phone abruptly stopped ringing. I gave one nod of my head and then tucked my arm in his, noticing for the first time that he was wearing something other than his stolid, professional suit. "*Très bon,* Sam. That tuxedo fits you perfectly, just as I knew it would. But haven't you forgotten your disguise?"

He laughed at me. "As if everyone there won't know who is on your arm for the evening. Regardless." He reached into his inner coat pocket and pulled out a small black half mask. "I didn't forget. I didn't want to put in on just yet."

"Yes, I know, you think my masquerade a frivolous thing. But it will be fun, I promise. Now let's go find the party."

Twenty-four

The Masque at Dangerous Crossings was already under way by the time Sam and I arrived. Like last year's party, it was supposed to be invitation only, but that idea only worked in theory. All of the public officials I dealt with on a daily basis needed to be invited; likewise, all Cadre members and the regular Crossings clientele. Adding in guests and friends of friends who'd managed to get their names on the list at the last minute, it was hardly an exclusive crowd.

Sam and I entered through the employee entrance; it wouldn't do for the hostess to be seen out of costume. Jules met us at the door looking rather uncomfortable in his pirate costume.

"Good evening, Miss Courbet, Dr. Samuels." He nodded and the golden earring looped into his left earlobe jiggled.

"You look wonderful, Jules," I said, reaching over and adjusting the bandanna that covered his curly brown hair.

He shrugged at my comment. "I feel silly."

I laughed. "But of course you do. That is the point of masquerades. Everyone feels silly, everyone looks silly, and so we all relax and let down our inhibitions. And women find pirates almost as devastatingly attractive as vampires, is that not right, Sam?"

Sam nodded. "It's the element of danger, the unpredictability of an unknown."

"See?" I said with a smile. "You cannot lose, *mon chou.* Now, how is the crowd tonight?"

"Restless," Jules said, "and anxious for the hostess to arrive."

"No doubt. I shall be ready soon. Has Monique come in?"

"Just a few minutes ago."

"Ask her if she will come back to Max's office and help me dress."

Jules walked away while Sam and I headed in the direction of the office. Max had been dead for years and still we all thought of this place as his. In truth, I found it hard to believe that he was dead; he had been a constant in my life for almost three hundred years, omnipresent, and at times I thought omnipotent. Max possessed so much power, lived for so many years. How could he allow it to end here, at the hands of one of his converts? It still made no sense to me. But for all of that, I was not sorry that he died. Quite the contrary, actually, I thought as I touched the brass plaque on the outside of the door. It hadn't happened soon enough. My only regret was that it had not been my hand to do the deed.

"May you rot in hell, you evil bastard."

"Excuse me?"

I started out of my reverie and smiled at Sam. "Nothing, my darling. Just an old lady's memories."

He laughed, his eyes running over my body like a caress. "As if you could ever be old, Vivienne. No matter how many years you have lived."

"*Merci,* Monsieur Samuels." I inclined my head to him and entered the office. Once it had been furnished entirely in black leather and chrome, but I had redecorated the interior when my sister came into ownership. I had even gone as far to renovate the small secret room behind the wardrobe mirror. Max had used it, I assumed, as a safe and secret haven. There had originally been two coffins stored there, one with his name on it and one with the name of Dorothy Grey. Max's had been put, finally, to its proper use and he had been buried in it. Deirdre's was still in her room in Cadre headquarters. Last I had looked, she was using it to store clothing. I felt a sudden rush of affection for her, irritating though she was at times.

"I wish, Sam, that you had managed to get Mitch and Deirdre to stay. At least for this night so that they could come to my party."

I opened the wardrobe door and pulled out my costume, neatly sealed in plastic wrappings. Sam craned his head to see and I put it back and closed the door again. "No," I said, giving him a little tap on the wrist, "you must not see it beforehand. It would be bad luck."

Sam laughed. "I think that is only for weddings, Vivienne."

"Oh, you are right, of course." I walked over to the bar. "Would you like a drink, *mon cher?* Fortification before we greet the crowd?"

"That would be good, thank you."

I busied myself, opening a bottle of wine and

pouring two glasses. There was a rustle of paper and when I turned I saw that my desk now contained a few brightly wrapped presents. "And it needed only this, Sam, to make me feel an old lady. Who told?"

Monique spoke from the doorway. "I did, Vivienne. You didn't think that you could escape the birthday celebrations again this year, did you?"

I sighed. "It is not really my birthday, you both know that."

Sam gave me a kiss on the cheek. "It's as good a day as any to celebrate it, though, especially with the party already being prepared. Besides, Vivienne, I know how much you adore presents."

"True." I sat down and looked at the packages. "Which one shall I start with?"

Sam walked over and pushed the smallest box in my direction. "Open this one first. Deirdre gave it to me when I drove them to the airport last month. And I have been keeping it secret ever since."

"Ah, my dear little sister." I pulled off the paper and opened the box, laughing when I peered inside at the necklace of bats and red stones. "Priceless." I held it up to show the others. "Where on earth did she get it?"

"I don't know," Sam said, "but she told me to tell you that they are 'creatures of the night. They fly.' "

Giggling, I clasped the necklace around my throat, then turned my attention to the other three presents. "Which one now?"

Sam handed me a small square packet. "Claude gave this to me earlier."

I smiled. "I am sure I know what this is." And

when I opened it, I found that I was right. A New Orleans blues collection. "Very nice," I said, "I will have to thank him for this later. Where is he?"

"He's been watching the door," Monique said. "There were a great many people trying to get in without invitation and Jules thought he'd be a good doorman."

I laughed. "Now which one is next?"

Sam handed me the largest package this time. "This one is from me."

Savagely, I attacked the paper. "Ooh," I said as I saw what was inside. "A laptop computer? Thank you."

I read the box; it might as well have been written in Greek. Although since I did speak some Greek that would have been more comprehensible than the phrases that were printed there. "I love it," I said with a grin. "There is something so unconventional about giving a three-hundred-year-old vampire a computer for her birthday."

He looked a bit disappointed at my response.

"Oh, no, Sam. Do not pout, *mon cher.* I love it," I said again. "It was very sweet and thoughtful of you. Not to mention, modern. But whatever shall I do with it?"

"You'll learn how to use it, that's what. It's archaic, the way you've been running an organization and a business without one. Trust me, Viv, you'll like this as much or more than VCRs and vampire movies."

"I am sure I will." I got up from the desk and gave him a long, passionate kiss, to make up for my somewhat lukewarm reception of his gift. He leaned into me and returned the kiss, running his hands up my back and holding me close.

I practically purred with the pleasure of his warm touch. "I will thank you better later, *mon cher,*" I whispered to him, "when we are alone."

Monique cleared her throat and we separated. "There's one more, Vivienne," she said, holding the last box out to me. "This one's from me. But perhaps, Sam, you could leave us alone, so that after it is opened, we can dress for the party?"

"No problem." He gave me a quick kiss and went to the door. "I'll go tell them to start the music."

After the door closed behind him, I smiled at Monique. "Thank you for remembering."

She shrugged. "It was nothing." Then she gestured with the box. "Do you want to open this?"

"Absolutely." I tore the wrappings from it eagerly, then stopped in amazement when I saw the contents: a small oil painting of a blond-haired girl standing naked by an open window, moonlight pouring over her pale skin and illuminating that which she was studying outside. I knew the scene well, having stood at the same window, although the artist had taken liberties with the location. Place du Carroussel had never been visible from my window in the House of the Swan. But still, it was a legitimate conclusion. The girl of course was I and the painter was . . .

"Eduard." The name escaped my lips in a whisper; it was a name I hadn't allowed myself to speak aloud for centuries, no matter how often I thought it. Running my fingers gently over the paint, I closed my eyes and pictured his strong hands gripping the brush, remembered also the touch of those hands on my body. I sighed, not meaning to. "Ah, dear Eduard."

Monique smiled, the tips of her canines peeking over her lower lip. "Yes, it is one of his. As soon as I saw it, I knew you had to have it."

"But where on earth did you find it?"

She shrugged. "Our last trip to Paris, remember? There was an antique dealer right outside of the hotel."

"And that is where you kept disappearing to? Your big secret?"

Monique nodded.

"And here all along I thought you had a lover stashed away somewhere." I set the picture on the desk and moved toward her, giving her a hug and a kiss almost as passionate as the one I'd given Sam. "Thank you, *mon amie.* There is nothing to compare to this. But it must have cost you a pretty penny."

"Actually." She pulled out of my arms. "It didn't cost me all that much. The antique dealer"—Monique gave me one of her devilish smiles—"proved very cooperative. So you weren't too far wrong with the lover theory. Anyway, I thought you'd like it. Now let's get dressed for the party."

Monique was ready much sooner than I, having picked a simple Egyptian tunic and headdress to wear. It suited her well, I thought, her tall, lithe body almost glowing through the sheer gauze material of the dress. With the addition of a little bit of gold jewelry and a gold half mask she was done while I had hardly donned the first of my voluminous petticoats.

"Whatever was I thinking," I said as I twisted around to fasten the ribbons at my waist, "when I chose this costume?"

"You were thinking about the past. And that is

always a mistake." With a laugh, Monique came up behind me and began to help me dress, fastening the tight bodice and smoothing the outer skirt down over the many layers of net, lace, and wire hoops.

"It is strange," I said, wiggling my shoulders about, trying to get comfortable in the tight sleeves, "that we once wore all these clothes and never gave them a second thought."

"Hold still," Monique murmured, her hands twisting my hair up onto the top of my head and fitting the feathered hood around my face. "And voilà, you have once again become *Mademoiselle Cygnette.*"

I picked up my mask from where it had fallen to the floor of the wardrobe. It too was adorned with white feathers, and the handle was covered in white velvet and trailed satin ribbons. Standing in front of the mirror I appraised my appearance. Staring back at me was a pale girl seemingly covered in feathers. My gray eyes looked enormous and almost black in the sea of whiteness. I turned my head from side to side, then looked over to Monique. "Some rouge, do you think?"

"No, I don't think. You look glorious just the way you are. I just hope you aren't planning on feeding in that getup. A drop of blood would ruin it."

I threw my head back and laughed. "Oh, Monique, you know as well as I do that nothing can be ruined by blood. But I fed well last evening, so you need not worry." I turned around and craned my head about to see the back. "It is very like that other one, isn't it?"

"Almost exact, I'd say. Except, of course, for

that silly headdress. Although why you'd choose to wear it again . . ."

I shivered slightly. Why had I chosen this costume again? Not that it carried such horrible memories; no, I had worn such clothing on one of the happiest nights of my life. And yet I had always made such an effort not to dwell in the past, not to try to regain days and years long lost.

"Prenez garde à la fuite du temps," I whispered too quietly for her to hear. "Just lately, Monique, I feel that the past is stalking me; that I am the prey and others, unknown, are the hunters. I feel that all of my years blend in with each other so that I hardly know what is the present and what is the past. It is frightening and I do not know how to fight this feeling."

Monique shrugged. "You are under pressure, *mon chou,* that is all."

"Is it? I wonder. . . ." I made a concerted effort to swallow the past, to bury it deep within so that it could not reemerge. Then taking a deep breath, I lifted my mask to my face and smiled, making a small curtsy to the mirror and to Monique. "The past be damned, we are here now. It makes no difference how we arrived at this moment." I giggled a bit as I moved toward the door. "Let's party."

Twenty-five

Dangerous Crossings looked festive for once, less like a dungeon and more like a ballroom. Perhaps it was the bright colors of the costumes, perhaps it was the electric candelabra I'd found in storage in the basement and had hung on the walls, although they in themselves were rather ominous, being hands holding the electric candles. Still, the extra bit of light helped brighten the atmosphere as did the hundreds of balloons floating above the dance floor, dangling glittering streamers.

Sam had met me at the door to the club; Monique gave my hand a brief squeeze. "You don't need to have me ruining your entrance; after all, it's your party," she said and quickly disappeared in the sea of bodies.

Sam cleared his throat, watching her leave. "That's quite a costume she's almost wearing. But you, Vivienne, you look radiant. Like an angel."

"A swan, actually," and I raised my arms to show him the wings.

"Of course, a swan." He pulled away from me briefly, inadvertently, then tucked my hand back into the crook of his elbow. I doubt that he was even aware of his reaction, that he realized the reminder of my alternate shapes was disturbing to him. A man of science, Dr. John Samuels could believe in vampires only because he could not deny the evidence. Vampirism was viewed and accepted by him as a disease, either of the body or the mind. It little mattered which since both could be easily adopted into his philosophy. But to accept and deal with the shape-shifting of which we were capable? No, he had not acted the same toward me since I'd exhibited the talent, treating me with just a little more wariness than before. It was not a good sign for our relationship.

Nor, I thought as we proceeded through the crowd to my special table, did I want it to be a relationship. I was not my sister and he was not Mitch.

No, what Sam and I had was convenient for both of us. Gone were the days when I needed a watchdog as Raoul or Rosa had been. Now I simply needed an escort, someone with whom I could make a memorable entrance. I had heard that he'd once referred to himself as "arm candy" and perhaps that wasn't too far off the truth. He was one of the most handsome men I knew in this most recent century, but it was more than that. I liked the man, I cared for him—he was a wonderful lover, he made me laugh, and he made me feel beautiful when I knew that the mirror lied.

I gave him a sidelong glance as we moved through the crowd and took our positions at my private table. And what did he get from me? Besides the vicarious thrill of escorting one of the most dangerous women he'd ever meet? I met his eyes and he smiled.

I had once asked him that very question. We had just made love and I was dressing to return back to my room before dawn. He lay on his side and watched me, his elbow resting on the pillow and his head propped up on his raised hand.

"Sam? *Mon cher?*"

"Hmm?"

"Why do you waste your time and your precious few years on a creature who can ultimately only mean heartbreak for you? As hard as I try, I am afraid I cannot see that we have any future with each other. You should leave me and find a nice human woman." He made a snorting sound at that comment, but I continued. "You should settle down and have children. And every year at Halloween, you can tell them about the vampire you once kept company with."

He laughed just a bit and gave me a sad smile. "They wouldn't believe me. Besides, I don't want a nice human woman. I'm happy with you."

"But why?"

He rolled over onto his back and stared up at the ceiling for a second before answering. "It's simple, Viv. And it's all about research, of course. How else will I be able to publish my study on the hemoglobinly impaired? You can't possibly think it has anything to do with you. You are just a guinea pig for my studies. I hope you don't mind."

I had kissed him then and walked back to Cadre

headquarters, shaking my head. *Research, indeed,* I'd thought, *there's more to it than that, my man.*

But I took his answer at face value. It didn't do to think too far ahead in a relationship with a human.

So I pretended my reasons and his reasons were all of the truth. That way we both received what we said we wanted. A perfect relationship that took us nowhere. In a hurry.

Jules came by and filled our glasses with champagne, bringing a plate of hors d'oeuvres for Sam to eat. From the platform on which our table sat, I watched the dancers, enjoying as always the closeness of so many humans. And for this one night, at least, the clothes were enjoyable as well. Ordinarily the clientele dressed in black almost entirely; it didn't matter what the garment was made of—silk or leather or vinyl or spandex—the color was always the same. Finding such conformity depressing, I took great delight in being different and breaking the chain by wearing something in pastel shades.

Tonight, though, I did not stand out in the crowd. I could mingle with them and not be recognized. And neither could anyone else; one of the thrills of a masquerade, I thought, was the complete anonymity it granted everyone.

I finished my glass of champagne and took Sam by the hand. "Dance with me," I said and we found a place on the dance floor. To my great delight, the band, chosen for their eclectic style and repertoire, began to play a waltz.

"Now this is dancing." I smiled up at him as

we twirled around. "Nothing like the half-crazed jiggling they do today."

He nodded indulgently.

"It's not fair, you know."

"What?"

"That you should be handsome, intelligent, sexy, and a good dancer."

"A plethora of riches?"

"Oh, yes."

I closed my eyes and let the music carry me along. The song ended all too soon, and as we turned toward the band, applauding them, Monique stepped up on the stage and took the microphone.

"Good evening," she said, "and welcome to the second annual Dangerous Crossings Masquerade. Some of you may know me as the shadow of our esteemed hostess, the vivacious Vivienne Courbet, a woman who needs no introduction. Except that I am going to give her one regardless. Vivienne?"

I shook my head and she laughed. "Can you believe it? She's suddenly shy, a personality trait no one would suspect." There was a small bit of laughter at this, including Sam's. "But I happen to know of another of her aspects that no one else does."

"What is she doing?" Sam leaned over and whispered. "What is she going to say? Is she drunk? Do you want me to get her out of there?"

"She isn't drunk, but don't worry. I think I know what she's going to say. And I'm going to kill her."

"I was at the band auditions," Monique continued, "and there I've discovered the one thing I had forgotten about Mademoiselle Courbet. She is an accomplished and talented chanteuse." She paused and looked straight at me. "Vivienne? Would you, please?"

"Only one," I said as I mounted the stage. There was a moderate amount of applause, not overwhelming, not even particularly encouraging. And I couldn't blame them for being skeptical; they had come for the open bar and the free food, not to hear me sing.

I looked at the band leader. "Do the one we did at the auditions."

I took the microphone from Monique and stuck my tongue out at her. "Thank you," I said as she moved off the stage. "You will pay for this later."

"But"—I addressed the crowd—"since I am here and you are here and we've all got to do something, I will sing my favorite song. Written by Monsieur Willie Nelson and with apologies to Mademoiselle Patsy Cline who is really the only one who can do this song justice. Although since she is dead, I'm sure she won't object too much."

The band began the short introduction, just keyboards and drums. And I sang. After the first few lines, people began dancing again and as they moved past the stage I recognized some of the couples. Monique danced with Sam, and Jules, with one of our waitresses. Even Claude was present; dressed as an impressive Cardinal Richelieu and amazingly light on his feet, he seemed to engulf an unidentified and tiny young woman dressed as a cat. When the song ended, the applause sounded more than polite. "It is a wonderful song, is it not?" I said and curtsied to my audience. "*Merci.*" I put the microphone back into its stand. "Enjoy the party."

At first I thought the noise from the back of the room was an overenthusiastic fan of my singing. But no, the voice sounded angry and harsh. Then I discerned the words.

"Death to the vampires of the Cadre."

From my vantage point on the stage I had a clear view of the club. The guests who knew what those words meant tensed and spun around to face whatever threat approached. A woman in a French maid costume screamed. A flash of black and red darted out the exit with the faint jingling of bells. "Give him room," someone else said. "Is there a doctor here?"

"Why bother?" said another woman, a note of choked hysteria in her voice. "He's got to be dead right now."

"Lock the doors!" I heard Claude's steady voice and was thankful he was here. "Do not let anyone leave. And yes, young lady, that means you. As well as your friend and the twenty people standing behind you. I have called the police and the paramedics and they will be here soon. Until then, everyone stay put and stay calm."

I stepped off the stage and the crowd parted for me, closing back in behind me.

Jules lay on the floor, a three-foot wooden stake protruding from his heart. My nostrils flared from the overwhelming scent of his blood. I heard one woman sobbing uncontrollably and someone else was vomiting in the corner. At least I was right about one thing; this would be a night to remember.

This made no sense. Why would anyone want to kill Jules? He had no enemies, he had been charming and well liked by club employees and Cadre members alike.

I knelt down next to him, not caring that the pool of his blood was being absorbed into the feathers of my costume. His eyes were wide-open in shock, his hands twisted around the stake as if he had attempted to pull it out before he died. I shivered, reaching over to close his staring eyes and smoothing back a lock of black hair that had escaped his once-jaunty pirate bandanna. "I am so sorry, *mon ami*. You will be avenged."

Twenty-six

"No," I said for what must have been the hundredth time that night, sitting behind my huge desk in Max's office. "I do not have a clue who might have done this. Jules had, to the best of my knowledge, no enemies and there was no good reason for him to have died like this. Why would you ask me to determine the purpose behind a madman's actions?"

The police had arrived shortly after the paramedics. Neither of them could have arrived soon enough to be of help to Jules, but the medics were wonderful at calming a hysterical crowd. The police were being less than helpful, I thought, spending entirely too much time questioning me and not near enough time trying to track down the murderer.

"Once again, Miss Courbet, do you know what the phrase"—and he consulted his notebook for the exact words—" 'death to the vampires of the Cadre' means?"

I stood up from my chair and leaned over my desk, glaring at him. "Of course I know what it means. I speak English easily as well as you. But as for why such a thing would be said? There are no vampires here, they are creatures who do not exist. So I can only surmise that the murderer is crazy."

"And the Cadre? What is that?"

The existence of the Cadre was not necessarily a secret. On paper we were a group of rich entrepreneurs; only one or two within the city government knew we were more than that. And I was determined to keep it that way.

I shrugged. "We have been over this, Officer, many times. Perhaps he was speaking metaphorically. Perhaps he saw all the costumes and really thought there were vampires within. Perhaps he had a pointed stick he wanted to try out. But I"—I walked over to the window and pulled the curtains open just a bit to check on the night sky—"I have no idea what he was thinking."

Dawn was a little more than an hour away, I estimated. And I could not stay here answering mindless questions until it arrived. Turning away from the window, I faked a yawn. "Now, if you don't mind, it is very late and I am very tired. I have lost an employee and a friend tonight, in a horribly gruesome manner. I suggest you leave me to my rest and attempt to make sure this does not happen again."

What could they do? There was absolutely no way I could be charged with this murder; the entire club was witness to my innocence. And there was no reason why I should be charged. Why they had lingered as long as they had here in my office asking questions I'd already answered was almost a bigger mystery than the crime itself.

Except that if they weren't stupid, and I didn't

believe they were, these men could certainly tell that I wasn't being entirely honest with them. It did not matter, I knew, especially when Sam came back into the room and nodded to me. The phone rang and I picked it up.

"Hello?"

"Vivienne? Do you have any idea what time it is, woman? And what the hell is going on?"

Every city government has at least one individual who, from his seemingly innocuous position, holds all the power and pulls all the strings. In New York City at this time it was James Christensen.

"Jim," I said, "I'm so sorry to have woken you, but I need your assistance. Perhaps you would like to explain to some of your officers that I am not a murderer."

"Oh, dear. I had heard about that, Vivienne, and you have my condolences. But why are they accusing you?" He made an exasperated noise. "Never mind, just let me talk to one of them."

I held the receiver out, waving it in the direction of the officers. "Mr. Christensen would like to speak with you."

The two officers exchanged a quick glance and seemed to stand a little straighter. "Yes, sir," the one who took the phone from me answered. "This is Sergeant DeMarco."

I could hear Jim on the other end of the line. "What the hell are you doing harassing Miss Courbet? I can assure you she didn't instigate this event. Get off your asses, get the hell out of there, and catch the bastard who did it."

"Yes, sir."

"And put her back on the line. Now!"

Sergeant DeMarco gave me a sheepish grin and handed the phone back to me.

"*Merci,* Jim," I said, "and aren't you sorry you missed the party?"

He gave a sleepy laugh. "Not at all, as a matter of fact. Is there anything else I can do for you?"

"No, thank you. Sleep well."

"You too, my dear."

I hung up the phone and looked over at the officers standing there. "Are there any other questions I can answer for you?"

"No, I'm afraid we've already taken up too much of your time. Thank you for your courtesy."

I waited until they were well out of earshot before I started to giggle. "Amazing what you can do with a phone call to the appropriate person. Thank you, Sam."

"My pleasure, Viv, as always. I rather enjoy riding to your rescue."

I walked across the room to him and gave him a warm kiss. "I feel rather guilty about it, though. They were only doing their jobs. And they knew I knew something I wasn't telling."

He shrugged. "You'd no other choice, Vivienne. It serves no good purpose for the general population to know what the Cadre is. Half of them wouldn't believe it and the other half would be sharpening stakes."

I shivered. "I can't believe this happened, Sam. What does it mean? And why Jules? Why not me? If you were privy to the secret of the Cadre, I would be the obvious choice to kill. Jules was a little fish."

Sam thought for a while. "Maybe the death wasn't the primary reason. It could be that Jules just happened to be in the wrong place at the wrong time. Maybe it was a message."

"But from whom? And why? So few people know we exist and we harm no one."

He smiled at that comment and I grew just a bit angry at him. "Damn it, Sam, you know that's true. We take so very little and we give back a lot. Look at all the Cadre money that's been given to charities—day care centers, housing for the homeless, soup kitchens—you name it, and we have supported it." I gave a bitter laugh. "Although it is true we do not do this for the most noble of reasons, we do do it. And that is what matters."

Sam nodded and looked at his watch. "Are you going back to Cadre headquarters tonight? If so, we'd better grab you a cab and get you there soon."

"No, I think I'll stay here for the day. Care to stay with me?"

He smiled. "And sleep with you in your coffin? I think not, sweetness. But thanks for asking."

"Oh, Sam. I wish you would stay." I ran my fingers up his cheek and through his hair, kissing the corners of his mouth. "There's a bed in there," I whispered persuasively, "as you well know."

He pushed me away. "I can't. As tempting as the offer is, I have some things I need to take care of tomorrow."

I pouted. "But I thought you said you didn't have to work tomorrow. Stay with me, Sam. Please."

He started to refuse again, but something changed in his expression. "What's wrong, Vivienne? I know that what happened with Jules was horrible for you and everyone else. But I have the feeling it is more than that with you. Talk to me. I'm a good listener, you know. It is, after all, how I make my living."

"If I knew, Sam, I would tell you. I have this haunted feeling and I'm not sure I can explain it. I have tried to live all my years without ever once looking back in regret or sadness or anger." I laughed, picked up the painting on my desk, and set it back down. "And it has always worked for me. No worries, no responsibilities, no tears—just me and *la joie de vivre.*"

"But in this last week it is as if . . ." I paused. "Oh, I don't know. I am no good at this self-examination, I fear. But that phone call this afternoon and this painting Monique gave me"—I ran my fingers over the frame—"the flash of a red and black costume on the dance floor, singing for the crowd, seeing Jules dead—all of it adds up to something and I do not know what it is."

His eyes searched my face. "Maybe it's stress. You've hardly taken any time off since you returned from Paris; you had this party to arrange, Cadre business, Dangerous Crossings business. All of that is more than one person can handle."

"That is what Monique said. But I've been in worse situations before and never felt this way."

"Maybe it'll go away. You're upset right now about Jules's death, which is perfectly understandable. You wouldn't be normal if you weren't."

Choking back the beginning of tears, I gave him a wan smile. "But I am not normal, Sam, and I am afraid. Something terrible is waiting. I do not know what it is, do not even know why it is there. But I can sense it on the edge of my senses, pacing back and forth, stalking me, mocking me."

I moved to where my costume hung over the wardrobe door—Jules's blood had been absorbed by the feathers, turning the skirt a dirty red almost to the waist. I plucked one of the feathers and held it to my nose, then laid it down on the desktop as if it were one of my birthday presents.

"Sam," I said, trying and failing to disguise the tremor in my voice, "do you believe in ghosts?"

He walked over and kissed me on the forehead. "No, sweetness, I don't." Then he stepped back, holding my arms. "And I don't think you do either. Get some rest, okay?"

Twenty-seven

I laughed as I showed him to the door. He was right, of course, I didn't believe in ghosts. And I was stressed and weary. No doubt things would look differently after a good day's sleep.

At the desk I pulled a ring of keys out of the top drawer, collected my presents, and unlocked the door behind the wardrobe. When Max had been alive, this room was no more than a concrete block cell, unlit, unfurnished, cold, and dank. I'd had the room wired and brought in decorators, so that it was now a serviceable area, comfortable and welcoming. I chuckled to myself; when telling this story to others of my kind, I always liked to elaborate and tell them that, of course, the workmen had to be killed after the job was done and that I had walled the dead bodies in behind the floral wallpaper. In reality, they had taken their money and left. I imagined they'd seen stranger sights.

In addition to my spare coffin the room also held a small bed, covered in a floral chintz that matched the decor of the office outside. I kept an assortment of clothes in the chest of drawers in one corner, and the built-in shelves at the end of the outside wall held a stereo system and CDs, a television, a VCR, and an assortment of tapes. I would rarely admit it, but I was hopelessly addicted to vampire movies. It didn't matter if they were good or bad or howlingly funny, I loved them all and watching them over and over was one of my secret narcissistic pleasures.

A large set of bookshelves held an assortment of titles, classics and contemporaries, most written in French. It was the first language I had struggled to read and despite all the years away from my country it was still my language of choice.

I took off the clothes I'd put on after stripping away my blood-soaked costume and pulled a pink silk nightgown from one of the drawers. As I slid it on, I wished that the room had been big enough to allow for a small bath. The smell of Jules's blood lingered sour on my skin and I longed for hot water to wash it away.

Instead I sprayed myself with some of my cologne, a special blend I had made in France, expressly for me: cloves and orange blossoms.

I locked the door then, scolding myself for not having done it sooner, then walked over and pulled the spread back on the bed, crawling in and flipping on the television with the remote control.

The morning news was on. And last night's events at Dangerous Crossings were the lead story. I sighed. My little masquerade party had turned into a nightmare.

I turned up the volume on the set. ". . . Miss Courbet, owner of the club and one of the city's most mysterious and eligible bachelorettes, was not available for comment."

"Damned straight," I said. "Nor will I be. And what is this nonsense? Bachelorette?"

It would have been the end of the story, but the anchorman turned to the newswoman. "So, Terri." He had an avid look in his eyes and I was surprised he wasn't drooling; it was such a juicy story. "This is not the first bizarre killing to happen at the site, is it?"

"No, Bob, you're right about that." She shuffled her papers a bit and straightened them out against the desk. "Before it became Dangerous Crossings, this particular club was called the Ballroom of Romance. And two people died in that club during that incarnation. Both of them by the hands of a NYC police officer in the line of duty."

"One of the deaths was a simple shooting, right?"

She nodded. "Yes, very cut-and-dried. A young man by the name of Larry Martin. He was apprehended while in the process of attempting to kill noted clothing designer Deirdre Griffin. Although"—she gave a smug smile, revealing perfectly straight white teeth—"Martin's choice of a murder weapon was, coincidently, a pointed stake."

"And the other killing?"

"The owner of the club at that time, Max Hunter, had been impaled on the door of his office."

"Yet another wooden stake, Terri?"

"It was actually the broken-off leg of a bar stool, Bob, but certainly close enough to a wooden stake to count."

"So what does this all mean to us now?"

She laughed. "It means that Halloween is over and has been over for a month. So put away your plastic fangs and your cape, or you may be next."

"*Merde*, such funny people." I clicked the OFF button on the remote with a violent flick. "Put *this* away, Terri," I said with a sneer.

I suppose it could have been worse. Regardless of the misfortune of the deaths they reported, the events were meaningless enough to them to relegate them to a joke. At least no speculations were being made about why, of all places, this club had such a history. No conjectures about why the method of killing was so archaic and reminiscent of bad horror movies. No headlines from the *New York Times* screaming VAMPIRES LIVE AMONG US! In truth, the Cadre paid big money in bribes to avoid this sort of publicity.

But they had gotten close this time—they were dancing around issues, pointing at coincidences one in the know could recognize as false. I took some consolation from the fact that this was a city in which all sorts of outrageous crimes were committed daily and today's hot news story often ended up as back page filler tomorrow. Yet, with enough hints and speculations, anything was possible; this story was filled with all the elements the public loved: blood, lust, and death. Not to mention the potential for hating those different. And I had learned over the years never to underestimate the depth of human prejudice for anything that deviated from the norm.

My hands went to the new necklace I wore, and, stroking the bats as if they were worry stones, I sighed. I missed Deirdre. And Mitch. Either of them would have known what to do; together they'd know what steps to take to avoid disaster. I missed Victor and his "listen to me or die" leadership that had always managed to sidestep complications like the one that threatened now to arise. Even Max might have had some good advice for me.

Then again, I thought, sitting up in bed and looking over at the bookshelves, *I do have advice from Max.* On the bottom shelf of the large bookcase was an entire set of black leather-bound journals authored over the hundreds of years of Max's vampiric existence.

I got out of bed, put in the new blues CD Claude had given me, and sat cross-legged on the floor, pulling out journals one by one and reading the first several pages.

It was fascinating reading. An incredible true story told by an incredible man. For while I disliked Max almost to the point of hatred, I could still acknowledge what he had been: a powerful and magnetic creature capable of so much I'd never have thought possible when I was human. Or even when I was a young vampire. I still could not understand how he had let himself be killed. Perhaps the answer lay in his journals.

The pages were brittle with age and the handwriting had faded. That, plus the fact that at least the earliest ones were written in archaic Spanish, made them difficult reading. If there existed an answer here, I was going to have to work for it.

"Typical Max," I said as I pulled out the next volume. "Never make it easy." I turned the pages slowly, giving each a perfunctory glance before moving on, until I caught a glimpse of my name, along with references to Victor and a group Max simply called the Others.

Paris, December 1792

We arrived in good time, with hours before sunrise. Victor went to prepare our normal quarters and I, to escape his company, went to walk the streets. I passed the House of the Swan but did not go in. I would save that visit for tomorrow evening when there was more time. Plus, I must admit that I fear meeting Vivienne again. Does she still hate me, I wonder, for the death of Diego? Or is she willing to let the past remained buried?

I find it strange that I should care. What difference could her low opinion of me make? I detest Victor and yet we are still together despite that fact. The ties between maker and created are very strong.

The atmosphere of the streets is tense, fear hovering over the buildings and the people like dark storm clouds. And I feel that presence Victor has come looking for. The Others, as he calls them, are here, manipulating the existence of all who dwell in this city. There is indeed a curious crackle in the air, like lightning making ready to strike, a certain bone-chilling excitement, akin to that felt while transforming to another physical shape. If I can believe Victor's assessment that this is proof of their existence, then they must exist.

He would like to recruit them, to join our powers with theirs. I would prefer to leave them to their own devices. What they do to humans makes little difference to me; even should the frenzy of the revolution the Others have purportedly stirred and incited cut off every other head in France, it will not affect me or my life.

No, I am not here for a cause, not here to support Victor's move to unite vampires under a common goal. I have more power surging in my blood than I ever wanted to have, I have no wish to associate for all eternity with those of my own kind.

No, I did not come with Victor for any of those reasons. I came to make peace with Vivienne, if it is possible. And to remove her from the potential danger of this revolution if she will allow me.

I smiled. "That is very sweet of you, Max." Then I laughed. "Although I remember at the time I thought you were being an interfering bastard." I paged forward. Much of what was written were descriptions of Paris and the rooms in which he and Victor always stayed. And the many feedings he had made. His hunger must have been greater than mine, he seemed to need the blood every night. Or perhaps it was a desire.

Paris, December 1792

I must admit after seeing Vivienne again that she is a magnificent creature, a fact I manage to forget when not confronted by her. She has agreed to let the issue of Diego lie buried with his remains. But now I find that I do not like her current choice of companions. Perhaps I am just a jealous old man, a father for whom no person can be found acceptable for a much beloved daughter. But it is more than that. Monique does not ring true. And this Eduard that I keep hearing of? I dislike him already, intensely. Both of them seem to have some hold over my perfect little swan. Oh, how she would laugh if she knew that is how I think of her. Even before we attempted her change to her winged form, I knew that a swan was what she would be.

So I shall attend her masque and meet this Eduard. And then I will decide what is to be done.

"What is to be done?" I said the words aloud, not liking what they implied. Could Max have had something to do with Eduard's death?

I shook my head. Even if it were true, there was nothing I could do. Both of them were dead, buried, and out of my life.

I am not entirely sure that I wished it otherwise.

I put away Max's journals and turned out the light. The enclosed space of my coffin was a comfort; the lavender-scented satin sheets were soothing. I slept.

Twenty-eight

And I woke. Better rested, but none the wiser. As always my sleep had been deathlike: deep and dreamless. If I had hoped that reading Max's journals would trigger a response, help filter those cryptic messages from my subconscious, and subsequently solve all my problems on wakening, I was a fool. A fool who never dreamed.

I'd asked Sam about this once.

"I do not dream anymore, Sam. In fact I can hardly remember what it is like to dream, it has been so long."

He looked at me in disbelief. "That's not possible, Vivienne. Everyone dreams. You just don't remember them, that's all."

"I remember everything else in my life, Sam. Can my dreams be so terrible that they must stay buried deep inside me?"

He laughed. "Or maybe they're so good, your mind doesn't want to ruin your waking life."

I rolled my eyes. "How could anything be that good when I love every part of my waking life? Unless, of course," I hinted with a twisted smile, "they were dreams of you and me and . . ."

"Forget it, sweetness. I have to take a shower and get to work; I'm on the night shift tonight."

I followed him into his bathroom and watched as he undressed and got into the shower. He turned on the water, stepped into the tub, then looked over at me, holding the curtain open. "Do you want to come in?"

"No, *mon chou*, you like the water too cold."

"Good." He pulled the curtain shut. "You like the water entirely too hot."

I gave a soft laugh. "So what does it mean if I don't dream?"

"What?"

I raised my voice so he could hear me over the rush of the water. "What does it say about me if I don't dream?"

"It says you're one crazy lady, Vivienne. But I already knew that. And I love you anyway."

"No," I had whispered as I walked out of the room, "do not love me, Sam. That is the one dream I do not want. And cannot have."

I opened the coffin lid and peered out. The bedside clock indicated that it was about fifteen minutes or so past sundown. Stretching, I climbed over the side of my box and went to the dresser, from which I pulled out a pale blue sweater, a pair of panties, and a pair of black jeans. With the clothes tucked under my arm, I unlocked the door that led to my office, and from there walked out into the hallway, toward the employees' lounge. I knew that I would meet no customers and precious few staff members after the announcement last night that Dangerous Crossings would be closed until further notice due to the police investigation in progress.

"I really must have a bath installed down in my office," I said, entering the female employees' area so that I could finally take a shower.

Sam was right about the water temperature. I turned it up just as high as I could, in the hopes that it would warm my cold blood for a while, and as I soaped and shampooed and rinsed, I hummed the song I had sung for everyone last night. It was still one of my favorites, although now every time I heard it I would think of Jules.

And there's nothing wrong with that, I thought, *it is as good a memorial as anyone could get.*

Turning off the water, I reached for a towel on the nearby set of hooks and dried off. I pulled my sweater over my head, then wrapped another towel, turban style, around my wet hair and finished dressing.

On my way back to the office, I detoured to take a look at the main room of the club. It had been cleaned since the party, and there was nothing out of the ordinary left to illustrate the extraordinary events, except for the festive streamers still hanging down from the few balloons the cleaning staff had missed and the small area cordoned off by yellow emergency tape. *An interesting juxtaposition,* I thought as I watched one of the balloons descend slowly from the ceiling and bounce once against the floor. I wondered again why this had happened.

". . . A message," Sam had suggested, and perhaps that was true. And if so, would there be another such message? And would they keep getting delivered until we were all dead?

And why should anyone bother?

"What the hell do you want?" My voice filled the quiet room and was answered only by a high-pitched screech coming from the farthest corner of the bar.

"Who's there?" Two voices said the words in unison and I tensed. Another messenger?

"Show yourself," I said and again another voice spoke over mine but I relaxed slightly when I thought I recognized it.

"It's me, Vivienne. It's Claude. I am so glad to see you escaped!"

"Where are you?"

I peered out into the club. Other than a heavy patch of darkness near the bar, I could see nothing.

"Here. I'm here. Hiding."

And out of the darkness, his face swam into view. I gave a huge sigh of relief. "You idiot, Claude, I am pleased to see you but you scared the hell out of me."

As he came closer, I got a better look at him. And yes, it was Claude, but . . . "*Sacre bleu, mon cher,* what has happened to you?"

One side of his body was badly burned, the skin peeling away in thick layers from those areas that were not covered by clothing. "I went outside in the sun." Barking out a harsh laugh, he shrugged, causing the glass of liquid he held in one hand to slosh over onto his burned skin. "Damn!" He dropped the glass and it broke into pieces at his feet. "It was a shame, I know, to take such a risk and ruin my otherwise rugged good looks. But"—and he lifted the bottle of whiskey he had grasped in his other hand and took a quick hard swallow—"this is preferable to what happened to the rest of them."

"The rest of them? Claude? What on earth are you talking about?"

He peered at me through squinted eyes. "You don't know?" he asked.

"Don't know what?"

"Ah." He took another swig off his bottle and looked at me. "Have some."

"No, thank you anyway. It is not my choice of drink—"

"It was not really a question. Have some. It will help dull the pain."

"Pain? I am not in pain."

"Not yet, in any event. Can we go back to your office? I'd like to sit down."

I gestured with my hand that he was to proceed me and he did. I followed his huge, hulking form down the hallway and back into my office. It was not politeness to let him go ahead of me; he was acting so strange I did not want to turn my back on him.

When we entered, he headed straight for the couch, settled in on the couch, and drained the last half of his bottle in what seemed one long gulp.

"Another?" I went to the bar without waiting for his answer, opened a new one of the brand he had been drinking, and poured myself a glass of red wine from the carafe that I kept filled.

I pushed the bottle at him and watched him drink, while I took the towel from my head and shook out my damp hair. When he seemed calmer I spoke again. "So? Can you tell me now, Claude? I think I need to know."

He sighed and pulled a handkerchief out of his pocket to wipe his face. Then he winced as he pulled the fabric away and saw that a long strip of skin had attached to it. He gave another harsh laugh. "Victor would have said it served me right. I always annoyed him with the gesture."

"Claude?"

"It will heal, don't you think?"

I walked over to him and took his chin in my hand, turning his head so that I could assess the damage. Even now I could see that the skin beneath the blackened burnt areas was pale and healthy. "Yes, it will heal. Your rugged good looks, as you say, will return in a day or two. Unless you do not tell me right now what happened and I am forced to scorch the rest of your skin off of your body."

He sighed. "I am sorry, Vivienne. It's just that if I don't say the words, then it might still not be true." He took a long drink.

"Cadre headquarters is gone."

Twenty-nine

"Gone? How do you mean gone?"

"An explosion, around noon. News reports say that it was a terrorist attack. Or an inside job. Depending on which station you are watching. Basically no one really knows yet what happened, except that it did. The carnage was terrible." He licked his cracked lips and dabbed at his face again with his handkerchief. "Like one of those horribly graphic war movies. Smoldering body parts everywhere." He gave his head a violent quick shake as if to dispel the visions. "And those who survived the blast and hadn't the sense or the wits to seek shelter elsewhere burst into flames."

His voice trailed off and his eyes teared up.

I reached over and patted his hand. "How many others besides you survived?"

He shook his head. "I don't know, Vivienne, I just don't know. And there's no way to tell, really. Some of the bodies didn't necessarily have to be one of us. Even a human caught in that explosion would burn and shatter. I do not want to think that I'm the only one who made it. But it's been almost five hours since the blast, the sun's been down for at least half an hour, and I would think that the survivors would make their way here. It was the only place I could think of to run to."

He gave me a look out of the corner of his eyes. "I really thought that I had lost everyone, even you. But you were not there. So maybe others were not there as well. And maybe they have not yet heard the news."

"Claude?" A horrible thought struck me, one I did not want to give voice to.

"Yes?"

"Did you see Monique?"

"Yes."

"And so she is safe? Why didn't she come here with you?"

His face twisted up and he began to cry. Red-tinged tears streamed down his face and he made no effort to pat them off. "She's gone, Vivienne."

"No."

"She's gone, Vivienne. I saw her. She ran out of the wreckage ahead of me, burst into flames, and fell to the pavement. I wanted to get to her, to save her, but when my own skin began to smolder, my self-preservation instincts must've kicked in. All I could think of was to run and hide from the sun."

"Not Monique." If I said it long enough and strong enough, then it would be true. And she would not be dead. "Oh, please, oh, please, not Monique." The words were a wail of anguish and a prayer. "Not Monique."

"I'm sorry, Vivienne. There was nothing that could be done. She's gone."

A great torrent of anger rose up within me and

I could find no words with which to express it. Instead I found myself transforming into my white lioness form; no words were needed for this aspect of myself to show her rage.

I do not know how others of my kind see their transformations, as they are extremely private experiences rarely shared with anyone. But I visualized the events, as if standing outside of them and watching, in my human form, while still a part of my consciousness lingered in the creature into which I had changed. As if seeing through two sets of eyes, I both saw and acted upon my anger, slashing furniture, draperies, gouging out huge sections of the desk, the bar. Claude sat on what was left of the sofa not moving, not speaking, barely daring to draw a breath. He was smart in this. It did not pay to interfere.

When I had finished, I gave a great leap across the room and landed on top of my desk. I opened my mouth and a huge howling roar came out. Claude covered his ears and shivered.

And then the rage passed. Or more correctly the need to express it was gone. Deep within me, the anger still burned on and I intended to feed my enemies to its ravaging, deadly flames.

The lioness stretched, shaking off the tattered remains of my clothing. A shudder ran under her pale fur. And in just a split second I found myself crouched on the top of my desk, naked and shivering. Claude remained where he was, staring straight ahead, not moving a muscle.

I gave a bitter laugh as I went into the back room for more clothes. "I am done, Claude, you can breathe now."

I turned on the television as I dressed. "You

can come in, Claude, if you'd like," I called out to him. "I want to see the news."

He squeezed his way through the narrow entrance, looking around. "Nice," he said, "much nicer than my hole in the Westwood."

"This place was just a cell when Max had it. Took a little bit of work to make it livable. It's serviceable; I just wish there'd been room for a bath." I couldn't believe we were making small talk about the decorating of my room at such a time. But it filled the empty spaces and made the tragedy seem less real.

He nodded. "Yeah, I can see that. But still it's nice. I should try to do something to make mine homier. But I'd always had that room over at Cadre—"

"Hush," I said, not to stop talk of the event, but because the news was starting and I didn't want to miss a word.

"Good evening, this is Bob Smith with the news. Our breaking story tonight—the bombing of one of New York City's finest restaurants, the Imperial. Terri Hamilton is at the site of the emergency. Terri?"

The view on the screen switched to the night street outside the restaurant. "Thanks, Bob. As you can see around me"—and the camera panned on the still-smoking wreckage—"this was one of the most devastating explosions ever witnessed in this city. Police are still not sure about the cause of the explosion, but they are sure"—and she began walking across the street to where there was a huge hole blown out of the sidewalk—"that the highest concentration of explosives was buried four or five stories below street level. And that when it went off at approximately twelve noon today it triggered a chain reaction from smaller devices hidden on different levels.

"At first it was thought to be a gas main explosion, but the possibilities now of this having been an accident are very remote."

"So this was a deliberate act?" Bob's voice sounded smug, as if he'd like to say that he knew it all the time.

"Yes, Bob. A previously unknown terrorist group calling themselves simply 'the Others' contacted police shortly after the blast to accept credit. We have a tape of their statement." She paused, looking at first confident and then confused, nodding to someone standing out of view of the camera and giving a nervous laugh to cover the silence. "We had a tape of their statement, but apparently we are experiencing technical difficulties with it."

"Damn." I whispered the word, then breathed a silent thanks to Max and his journals. At least we had a place to start.

"People of New York City." Terri was reading the terrorist statement now from a slip of paper she'd been given. Her hands trembled slightly. "In time you will thank us for this violence. We shall not rest until every last member of the Cadre is exterminated."

"Shit." I turned around and looked at Claude. He was now sitting on my bed, his hands pressed up against his damaged face. "Who the hell are these people, Vivienne?"

I held up a hand; the story was still running.

". . . found out that the Cadre, on paper at least, is a group of entrepreneurs who have been operating in New York City since at least the turn of the last century. Very little is known of them. Now rumors and speculations are flying about what this group really is. And as crazy as it may sound, ladies and gentlemen, it seems now that this organization is actually an international group of . . ." Terri paused, giving the next word its full effect. "Vampires."

I turned off the television and stood for a while staring at the blank screen. "That cinches it. It's over, Claude. It was such a wonderful life while it lasted. Now we'll need to pack up and move on. No more relying on the disbelief of humans; they have proof now. The dead bodies of our kind that they hauled away will no doubt tell them all they need to know."

The phone rang in the next room.

"Claude," I said calmly, "get that for me, will you? Tell them I'll be right there."

"Hello? Yes, Miss Griffin, she's here. Me? This is Claude. You remember me, don't you?" He paused. "So far as I know, just myself and Miss Courbet." He paused again. "Yes, it was as bad as the news reported, or worse. And no one really knows why this happened."

I walked out into the office and held my hand out for the phone.

"Here she is, Miss Griffin. Nice talking to you."

"Deirdre?"

"Hello, Vivienne. I see that Claude and his impeccable manners escaped the explosion. And I am so pleased that you are still alive. Mitch and I cannot believe this is happening; when we heard the reports we feared the worst. Who are these people and what do they have against the Cadre? It almost sounds as if they know who and what we are."

"They do, Deirdre."

I heard her make a whispered comment to someone else, I presumed Mitch, there with her.

"Mitch says hang in there, Viv. We're catching a plane there as soon as we can arrange it. Where will you be?"

"Probably at the club. We're at least protected here from the crowd. Everything is still sealed off from the murder."

"Murder? Now that is something I had not heard of."

"You remember Jules?"

I could hear the smile in her voice. "Oh, yes, the ever so handsome Jules."

I sighed. "Yes. But not so handsome anymore, I fear. Someone drove a stake through his heart on the dance floor of the club last night."

"Jesus." Deirdre took in a deep breath and I heard low whispers from her end of the line. There was a pause then and the next voice I heard was Mitch's. "Viv? Are you okay? And do they know who did it?"

"At this point, I think it is safe to assume it is this group called 'the Others.' Have you heard of them? Has Deirdre?"

"No. But if that is who is responsible, it's a bigger group than we can know and their members must be everywhere. I killed someone just the other night who tried to kill us. And Lily called to say that they'd attempted the same thing with her and Victor." He gave a small chuckle. "That girl is something."

"Victor. Of course. Damn it. Victor." I hit my forehead with the palm of my hand. "Victor knows."

"What?"

"Victor knows about the Others, Mitch. Meet us in New Orleans."

Thirty

New Orleans, present day

The bar was dark. And empty.

"Are you sure this is the right place, Claude?"

Claude set our luggage on the floor. Looking around, he pulled out a pack of matches to read the cover and nodded. "The sign out front said the Blackened Orchid, didn't it?"

"Yes, I think so."

"Then it's the right place."

A voice called out from behind the swinging kitchen doors. "We're closed right now. And I hate to be rude." The figure came through into the bar section. "But I wish you'd leave anyway."

I stood amazed. So this was Lily. A small girl, just about an inch or so taller than I, and she was painfully thin, with her red hair cropped so short it was almost a crew cut. But despite all the differences, it was like looking into the face of Deirdre. I shook my head and looked her in the eye. "I did not really believe them when they said you looked exactly like her."

"Well, they were right," she said, combing her fingers through her hair. "Now get out."

"Lily? You can't . . ." Claude moved up to the bar.

She laughed. "I saw you there, Claude. How on earth could I miss you?" She gave a little cry and leaned over the bar, reaching out and softly touching his burned face. "That looks horrible, does it hurt?"

He shrugged. "It's healing quickly."

Lily smiled. "Cool, isn't it? How that happens?"

I gave a polite little cough and she glanced at me, then looked back at Claude. "And since you are here, then this must be Vivienne Courbet. And I'm very pleased to meet her and to see you again, but still you'll need to leave. Victor." As she said the name her voice softened and I felt an ache rise up in my throat. "Well, he's not doing so well right now. After that attack the other night. You heard about that, right?"

"Yes." I gave her a smile. "And that is why we are here."

She turned to me and bared her teeth. "Oh, yes, you smile and lie very prettily, Vivienne. And ordinarily, I'd let myself be convinced. But you see, I heard from my mother and Mitch. You are here because you need Victor's help. But he's not going to be able to help you, not tonight and not if he gets upset again."

"Lily, if you would only let us see—"

"No way, Claude. It's not going to happen. I'm sympathetic to your cause, of course, and I sure as hell don't want any more raving terrorist lunatics breaking in here and threatening Victor with a pointed stick. These Others, whoever the hell they are, need to be stopped. But in all honesty, Victor will be of no use to you now. So"—she crossed her arms in front of her black T-shirt and looked me dead in the eye—"I suggest you take your cute little French ass out of here for now and I'll call you when he's able to talk."

I stared at her for a whole minute in disbelief. How dare she? Didn't she know who I was? Didn't my over three hundred years of life experience mean anything to her?

And then she smiled. "Please," she said, "he's really bad tonight. But he'll get better, he always does. And then we'll help."

I started to giggle and when she joined me the tension in the air vanished. "I apologize, Lily, I hadn't realized Victor was that bad."

She looked suspiciously close to tears. "Ordinarily, he's good. You'd never know he wasn't quite right from looking at him. You know, maybe better than any, how he is. Weren't you the one"—now her eyes were angry—"who had him confined at that Cadre place?"

I sighed. "It wasn't really my choice. And he really wasn't confined. I knew that. I doubt he harbors any bad feeling toward me on that count."

"True. He seems very fond of you. But just last night I heard him talking to Max. Max? What's that all about?"

"Do you not know?" I looked at her and raised an eyebrow. "Max was Victor's—"

"Oh, I know the story." She interrupted me and started lining up the glasses and bottles behind the bar. "Believe me, Vivienne, I know the story. But I'm scared if he sees you, it'll set all of those memories off again. He's stored up an incredibly large amount of bad memories. And sometimes he's not sure what is real and what is memory."

Lily kept fussing with the glasses until she knocked two of them over. "Damn it." She took out a towel and swept the mess into a wastebasket. Then she set the towel down and stopped to meet my eyes. "Don't you see?" she whispered. "He's all I have. I can't let him go."

I wanted to cross over the bar and give her a hug. I wanted to take her into my arms and kiss her and soothe her and tell her that everything would be all right. But I knew that was a lie. Hadn't I said the same thing to Monique countless times?

"I'm sorry," I said, "I do understand. Do you know where we're staying?"

She nodded and gave me a small wry grin. "My mother made me write it down."

I nodded. "Good for her. Call me. But do not wait too long. I have the feeling the Others will not be quite so concerned with Victor's well-being."

Claude turned to me as we climbed into our taxi. "What now?"

"Now, we lie low and hope Victor gets better before the Others manage to kill him. You can help me read through Max's journals in the meantime, just in case." I gave him my most rehearsed innocent smile. "I brought the last couple of hundred years' worth with me."

He groaned and I laughed.

"Where to?" the driver said, pushing the little meter flag down. The time began ticking away.

"The Hotel of Souls, please."

* * *

The hotel staff was waiting for us when we arrived and checked us in like royalty. Not surprising, really, since I owned a 75 percent share of the operation. But it was more than that. Many of the night staff were also members of the Cadre and all were worried that a similar incident could happen here. A legitimate concern, but since I had told no one but Sam that I was leaving the city, I thought that the hotel would be safe enough. Anyone who cared to investigate it could easily find out that there was a connection between this place and the Cadre, though, and so it wouldn't be safe for all that long. And neither would any of the other thousands of places owned by the Cadre or Cadre members.

"No place to run and no place to hide," I said to Claude on the elevator. "We are going to have to start living by our wits and our instincts again."

He flashed me a sad smile. "Some of us always have."

"True, but in the past few years, we all have gotten fat and complacent."

Claude laughed. "That may be true. But some of us have always been fat."

I looked over at him and smiled. I do not think he had any idea of the seriousness of this situation. Or perhaps he did and had the same attitude as I did. Whatever his feelings, I was grateful for his solid comfort. "I did better than I knew with you, Claude. Thank you."

He blushed and I laughed and the elevator door opened. The bellboy was waiting there for us with our luggage on a cart.

He checked Claude in first and then walked me through the adjoining door into the largest suite available. "This will do quite nicely," I said, giving him a twenty-dollar bill. "Thank you," and I hesitated on his name.

"Raoul."

What a fortunate omen, I thought, and smiled, liking him already. "Thank you, Raoul."

"It's an honor, Miss Courbet. You are aware, I'm sure, of the amenities of these rooms. But let me reacquaint you with the more pertinent features. The windows," and he pulled aside the drapes, "are fixed with heavy shutters so that the morning light will not disturb you." He opened the shutters now, showing me the clasps. "It's a lovely view," he said, "and many of our clientele prefer to keep them open at night, closing them only when they wish to sleep."

I nodded and he continued, gesturing toward the bathroom. "All of the water gauges are set to extra hot for your bathing pleasure. And"—he walked over to the foot of the bed, opening the large ornate chest—"should you require extra safeguarding, you will find this feature most acceptable."

"Everything is perfect, Raoul. *Merci.*"

"I'm happy you are pleased. And now let me get you settled in a little bit more comfortably."

I was perfectly capable, of course, of unpacking my own cases. But he was young and courteous and handsome and I liked the look of him in his red and black uniform.

I lounged on top of the bed and watched him unpack my case, neatly hanging up clothes on hangers and laying the rest into lavender-sacheted drawers. "So tell me, Raoul, do you like your job?"

He turned from where he was setting up the laptop computer I'd brought with me at Sam's suggestion. "Yes, I do. This place pays twice as much as every other hotel in the area. Which is, I suppose, why it's so hard to get a job here. But it was worth all the effort. Especially when one gets to serve beautiful ladies."

I smiled. "And do you work the nights exclusively or do you do day shifts as well?" My question was more than idle curiosity. If he worked days then he was human, serving here because he was what we called a donor. And I was hungry.

Never let it be said that Vivienne Courbet went to her doom on an empty stomach.

"I usually do the day shifts, Miss Courbet," he said with a sly smile, "but I switched with Louis for this week." He plugged in two of the cords from the laptop, one into the power switch and one into a phone jack. "And there, you are all set up and ready to go."

"Thank you, Raoul. You have been most helpful."

"Certainly." He started to open the door. "Oh, I almost forgot." He reached into his pocket and pulled out an envelope. "This fax came for you."

I glanced at it, from Sam most likely. *"Merci."*

Raoul put his hand to the doorknob, but turned around once again. "And should you wish to call for room service a little bit later on, don't hesitate to ask for me."

I watched him walk out of the room and close the door. "Delicious," I said as I got off the bed and went to the phone to dial Sam's number. As it rang, I looked in the mirror on the other side of the room. "Vivienne Courbet." I made a face at myself, rolling my eyes. "You are an evil, reprehensible woman."

Thirty-one

Sam had wanted to accompany us, but had been called back into the psychiatric hospital on an emergency.

"There's just no way now, Vivienne. All of a sudden everyone here has gone completely berserk. I have never, in all my years of practice, seen anything quite like it. It's almost as if someone threw a switch inside these people's minds. We've called the entire staff in to deal with it and I daresay no one will be leaving the building until it's all under control."

I had filled him in on everything that I could before we left the city, including the involvement of the Others and how it was likely that they'd ordered assassinations on both Deirdre and Mitch as well as Lily and Victor. "They seem to know everything we do, Sam. I'm not entirely sure what any of us can do to stop them. Unless Victor can help."

"I hope he can, Vivienne. I don't want to lose you, not like this, at least. I know it's inevitable that . . ." His voice had trailed off. Had I been with him, I'd have kissed him and told him he was being silly. But there was no way I could do that through the phone. And he wasn't being silly; instead his assessment of our relationship was uncannily accurate and that made me sad.

"Take the laptop with you, okay? I'll fax instructions to you later on at the hotel and you can at least set yourself up an e-mail account. The phone service here is down—we think some of the patients cut the wires—and the battery on this cell phone is starting to fade. At least the computers are still working—since they're newer, they run off of different lines brought in to the building at a different place . . ."

His voice had faded away. I had no idea how to set up an e-mail account or even how to turn the stupid laptop on. And he was expecting hourly updates via e-mail? *"Merde!"* I had slammed the phone down and called for Claude to get us a taxi to the airport.

Not surprisingly, there was no answer at the hospital. I sighed and looked at the laptop in disgust. It had taken me many years to get accustomed to talking on the telephone. And now there was this.

I opened the envelope that Raoul had given me. And read the instructions Sam had sent. Twice. I usually did not like admitting to my ignorance, but I seemed to have no choice.

"Change, Vivienne," I said to myself quietly as I walked over to knock on the adjoining room door. "Change and adapt—it's what keeps you alive." I knocked again louder this time and called, "Claude?"

"Yes?" He opened the door, patting the burned side of his face with a towel. He was wearing his pants with the suspender straps down and had only his T-shirt to cover his chest. Another towel was wrapped around his neck. I had interrupted his toilette, apparently. But when he pulled the towel down from his face, I noticed that the burned strips of skin were gone.

I put a hand up and touched his cheek gently. "Oh, that looks so much better."

He smiled. "And you can only imagine how much better it feels." He got a wicked glint in his eye. "I must confess, though, that I'm surprised and just a little disappointed in you, Vivienne."

No more Miss Courbet, I noticed. Good. Since we were two, and perhaps the only, survivors of the explosion, formality was hardly needed. "Why would you be disappointed, Claude?"

"I'd have figured you'd be still busy with the lovely Raoul."

I gave him a little slap on the arm. "He's for later, of course. Now, I have an important question for you."

"Shoot."

"Are you . . ." I paused. "Damn, what is that phrase?" I thought for a minute, then snapped my fingers. "Literate. Yes, that is it. Are you computer literate?"

"These days, who isn't?"

I laughed. "I am not, for one. But I am pleased that you know something of it. Could you help me? Sam has faxed me instructions but it seems to be filled with nothing but initials. ISP? IRC? What is that?" I shrugged and opened my arms wide in a gesture of helplessness.

"No problem," he said and pulled the chair out from under the desk, sitting down. His large hands practically obliterated the keyboard, but he was as agile here as he was on the dance floor.

By the time he was done, I knew enough to turn on the computer, initiate the auto-dialer, and send e-mail to the one and only address in my book. Sam had already set up an e-mail account for me and my address was, simply enough, vivi-ennecourbet at vampmail.com.

"No, no," Claude said for perhaps the hundredth time. "You can't write the *at* out. You need to put in the little symbol." And he showed me.

"Thank you, Claude."

"Now," he said, getting up from the chair and gesturing for me to sit, "you can surf the Web all night. Or all day if you keep your shutters closed."

I laughed and sat down. "I do not think so, Claude. But should I choose to do such a thing, how would I go about it?"

He showed me how to open the browser and search for things I wanted to see.

I giggled. "But this is delightful. I could find out almost anything, couldn't I? Just by typing a few letters?"

He gave me an indulgent smile. "Don't forget to close the shutters, Vivienne. Good night."

I nodded and waved a hand at him, barely hearing his laugh.

I clicked on the ADVANCED SEARCH button and typed the words *the Others* into the little box. There were literally millions of matches so I set about refining the search to a more manageable number. No matter how much I tried to cut the total down, it didn't matter. The words were too common and any attempt to pinpoint anything but the most recent news stories was wasted effort.

I wasn't sure what I expected. It wasn't as if international terrorists would set up their own Web site. But still I searched, becoming more and more frustrated.

Two hours later I threw my hands up in exasperation, when yet another likely choice turned out to be irretrievable. I looked at the clock by the bedside and turned off the computer, shaking my head. "Ridiculous," I said, "one could sit and starve and never realize it. And still never find what it is one is looking for."

Raoul was off duty by the time I called, but he had been waiting for me. "I'll be right up," he said.

"No, actually"—I looked around the room—"I'd much rather go out for a while. Would you be willing to serve as my escort?"

"Gladly. You don't need to ask me twice."

"Fine, I'll be right there."

I went into the bathroom and splashed hot water on my face, brushed my teeth, and combed through my hair. Then I changed into a skintight black catsuit, boots, and a fuzzy pink angora bolero jacket. Checking in the mirror, I nodded first, then smiled and blew myself a kiss. "Not bad for an old woman."

Raoul was waiting for me in the lobby. He'd changed into a pair of black jeans, a T-shirt, and a black leather jacket. "I'd almost given up on you," he said, as I got off the elevator.

"Would you believe me if I told you I'd lost track of time on the Internet?"

He held the front door open for me. "Sure. It happens all the time. Where to?"

I laughed. "Since this seems to be a night for new things, take me somewhere I have never been before, somewhere different."

We started walking down the street. Even in December, the air was warm and lush with a deep floral scent.

"And just how am I supposed to know where you've been and what you've done, Vivienne?"

The significance of his switch to my first name did not go unnoticed. He was in charge now. I reached over and tucked my arm around his. "Easily, Raoul. Assume I've seen it all and done it all and start from there."

"Perfect," he said, "I know just the place."

I peered inside the bar to which Raoul had brought me. It smelled of urine and vomit and whiskey. A hand-printed sign hung on the wall next to the door. EXOTIC DANCER WANTED. MUST BE WILLING TO WORK FOR TIPS. INQUIRE WITHIN.

"Perfect?" I gave him a dubious look.

He chuckled. "In that I'm almost a hundred percent certain you've never been here before, yeah, it is perfect. That was the criteria, as I remember."

"True. I should have been more careful in phrasing my request. But how was I to know you would take me so literally?" But I smiled to let him know that I was only joking.

We walked in and Raoul found us a corner booth, ordering a bottle of red wine as he walked past the bar.

"So," I said after we sat down, "what is special about this place?"

"For one thing, half of the women in here are really men."

I glanced around the room, then gave him a sharp look, unsure as to whether he was making a joke. "Really?" I asked cautiously.

"Really. Not a big deal, I'm sure, to someone like you." Apparently he mistook my tone, thinking I'd meant to be sarcastic when I was merely fascinated. I let it go.

"And?"

"And in about"—he looked at his watch—"oh, a half hour or so, the voodoo guy will show up."

"Voodoo guy?"

"Sure. This is New Orleans, remember. The home of voodoo. Although they call it different names now. It's fascinating, don't you think?"

A waiter approached our table, put down a little bowl filled with some sort of crunchy snack sticks. "Raoul." He nodded, setting the bottle of wine and two glasses on the table. "And a lovely little friend." He smiled at me. "New in town, honey? You don't look familiar. And somehow I don't think you're here to audition as a dancer. Too bad."

I laughed. "I'm not a dancer, I fear. And I'm not exactly new, Monsieur, but certainly not a resident. I'm only here for a few days and Raoul agreed to show me the sights."

"I'm sure he did." He winked at me. "And no wonder. Enjoy."

The wine was hideous and cheap. But I drank it, not wanting to hurt Raoul's feelings.

He, however, had no such problem telling the truth. "God, this stuff is horrible. I apologize, Vivienne. You must think I'm some sort of yokel or something bringing you here. But I assure you, the voodoo guy is worth it."

"I certainly hope so. For this I have given up an evening in my room all alone trying to find out how to make a million by selling e-mail addresses. Or searching for things that do not seem to exist."

He laughed and took another sip of his wine. "It sounds like you are finding New Orleans a little bit less than exciting. You should have been here a month ago."

"Oh? Why?"

"Halloween. This town may not be as sharp and modern as New York City, but we certainly know how to throw a masquerade."

I shivered, reminded of Jules. "Let us talk of something different."

"Sure thing. Or we could just leave and go back to the hotel."

"Later. I want to see this voodoo man you keep talking about. Is he any good? Or more importantly, is he for real?"

"He's good, yeah. Very good. But real?" He shrugged. "I'm not sure. Before I settled here, I'd have laughed at you for asking that question. I didn't believe in any of it. But now, ever since working at the hotel, I see things in a new light." He sat staring at the door for a minute. "It's a lot different than I ever thought. You know what I mean? All the supernatural stuff, it's a lot different than what you read in books. Or"—and he smiled at me and winked—"what you see on the Internet."

He looked back at the door and then at his watch. "Right on time," he said. "Angelo is here."

Thirty-two

I turned in my chair and stared toward the man who just walked through the doorway. He was old and wizened, with a two or three days' growth of grizzled beard and the most pronounced bowlegs I had ever seen. As he walked into the bar and started to a table, I caught a whiff of his scent—cheap whiskey and smoke.

"He certainly looks the part," I said to Raoul. "What does he do?"

"Buy him a drink and he'll tell your fortune. And if you pay him well enough, I've heard that he has other tricks. Talk around here is his spell repertoire is the biggest in New Orleans. Just don't ask him about Greg. We've all heard that story more than enough times."

He smiled, though, and I could tell that he had great affection for this man.

"Let's buy him a drink, shall we?"

He stood up and waved to Angelo to catch his eye. The man chuckled and nodded, walking to our table.

"Raoul. An' a sweet little *fille*. What can I do for you, my boy? Seem to me you got everythin' you need here already."

"Vivienne would like to have her fortune told, 'Lo."

He slapped his knee and gave a huge guffaw. "Boy, you know nothin', that for sure. Woman got a face like this one, she don' need her fortune told. But for a glass of gin, I do it, you know I do it." He tapped Raoul on the shoulder. "Come on, Raoul, slide outta there, get goin', and get that gin while I make friendly with Miss Vivienne here."

Raoul looked at me questioningly.

"I am fine, Raoul. Go get the man his drink."

He moved out and Angelo sat down across from me. "Give me your hands, Miss Vivienne." He chuckled to himself about something. I held my hands out, palms up, and he took the left one into his hands. "You can put that other one down now," he said, "I got the one I need."

He stared at my palm for a while, then turned it over and looked at the back of it.

"You don' really want your fortune told, do you?"

I shrugged. "You can do it if you wish. I won't believe what you have to tell me anyway." And I laughed to soften the words. "It is not that I don't believe in you, you see. It is that—"

He finished my sentence. "You prefer to make your own fortune. Very wise, Miss Vivienne. But one as old as you should be wise."

I jumped, pulling my hand back from him. "How can you know how old I am, Angelo?"

"In your case, pretty lady, the years are in your eyes. And"—he tapped himself on the side of the head—"this ol' bokor has ways to tell."

"Here you go, 'Lo." Raoul handed him a small glass filled with gin. "Just the way you like it."

He bolted it down. "Thank you, young Raoul. Now make yourself disappear for a while. I need to ask Miss Vivienne some questions."

I nodded to Raoul and he went back to the bar. I watched him for a second, then shrugged.

"Now," Angelo started, "I can see you had a long life so far; maybe more than you should have. And you keep on losin' those you care for."

He leaned a little bit closer to me. I could smell the gin on his breath. "But what you don' know is that these people ain' necessarily gone." He gave a wheezing laugh. "No, they ain' very far from you at all." Then he grew serious and grabbed my hands again, gripping them tightly. His voice grew softer, but as he continued to talk, it was all I could hear.

"There's one there as blond as you. I catch hisself starin' at you over the long years. He not quite the same man he was, there somethin' diff'rent there in him. Somethin' powerful and evil—growin' and reachin' and graspin' for more than he should. Oh, this man, he want and he want and he never rest.

"And a dark-haired girl, she there too with him. Starin' at a dead baby and a glass full of blood. She love you if he let her, but don' you know, he won'. There be no love in this man. No love for you, no love for her, no love for that dead baby. A cold man. He not like me, Miss Vivienne. And no, not even like you. He somethin' diff'rent, somethin' new. Somethin' *other* than what he should be."

I gave a nervous laugh. "That is all very interesting, Angelo, and I did know a blond-haired man and a dark-haired girl, but they are dead."

"There's dead and then there's dead. And some don' rest as well as others. And I shouldn't have to tell such as you about such as that, should I?"

"So what should I do?" I didn't actually ask the question of him, but he answered anyway.

"For now, you can take that boy Raoul back to your room and each of you get what you need. Ain' love, but it do you for now. Then you can seek out trouble and look for the blond man and the dark-haired girl. Or you can do nothin' and they will seek you. One thing I know for sure, it be better if you find them first."

He slid out of the seat then and stood up, smiling at me. "No matter what you think, Miss Viv, you a good woman. A little like a diamond and a little like a rose. I wish you love and a life no longer than you can be happy in." He kissed my cheek, laughed, and walked away.

Raoul came back. "That was quite a fortune. What did he say?"

I shrugged. "You know how these people are, Raoul, they hit on a few specifics that apply to everyone and hint wildly at everything else." It was such a blatant lie that I couldn't look him in the eyes. But he accepted my answer.

"What would you like to do now?"

"Take me back to the hotel."

Raoul was as sweet as I had thought he would be—an ardent lover, confident and skilled, he explored my body with great enthusiasm, welcomed my bite at his neck, and did all the right things in the proper order. But I was out of sorts, distant and distracted. He rolled off of me finally with a sigh.

"You do know, Vivienne, that this exercise works better when both parties are present." He reached over and stroked my cheek with the back of his hand.

I gave him a twisted smile. "I have heard that. I'm sorry, Raoul, it was nothing you did. Or did not do. It is I who has the problem."

"We could try it again tomorrow," he said a little too eagerly. "Maybe after a good day's rest you'll feel differently."

"Perhaps. We shall see."

He laughed. "That was a no. I've heard that phrase before." He leaned over and kissed me full on the lips. "If you change your mind, call me."

After he dressed and left with another kiss, I got out of bed and locked all the doors and windows, fastening the shutters tightly. Then I took a long hot shower, put on my nightgown, and lifted the lid on the coffin at the foot of the bed, looking inside. It looked comfortable enough, but I wondered how it would feel to sleep in the open, without those confining walls around me. Dropping the lid, I turned out the lights and crawled back into the bed. The sheets were still warm and smelled of Raoul, a comforting human scent. I fell asleep quickly, not even giving myself time to ponder what that Angelo had said.

Thirty-three

I woke up in a state of panic, completely unaware of where I was. The room was pitch-black, with the only exception being the glowing numerals of the bedside clock. Glancing at it, I relaxed and remembered. I was in my room in the Hotel of Souls, New Orleans. And it was past sundown.

Sleeping outside of the coffin seemed to have done me no particular harm. I felt well rested and relatively prepared for what the night might bring. Stretching, I rolled over a bit and smelled the pillow next to my head. The scent of Raoul was fainter now, but still there. But it wasn't as much of a comfort as it might once have been. I thought for a while about why this might be. Was I growing so old that I was losing my passion?

As I stretched again I put my hand under his pillow and touched something dried, something scratchy. I pulled it out and saw that it was a bundle of lavender and violets tied in a red satin ribbon. I smiled. I didn't remember him buying this; he must have snuck it in while I wasn't looking.

Across the room a little green light was flashing,

indicating a voice mail waiting. I jumped out of bed, thinking it might be a message from Sam.

And I stopped, midway between the bed and the phone. Sam? Could it be that I was missing him more than I'd expected? Could it be that I cared for him more than I knew? It could very well explain my reaction to Raoul last night. Not a lost passion, then, but a directed one.

I picked up the phone and pressed the MESSAGE button. To my disappointment it was not from Sam. "Viv? It's Mitch. We're here, stupid bloody airlines lost Deirdre's bag and we almost had to spend the day hiding out in rest rooms in the airport. Fine thing, that." He laughed. "Nice hotel, by the way." There was a pause. "Oh, Deirdre says we'll meet you in the lobby bar around seven or so. She talked to Lily and . . ."

There was a beep and the message was over. And he hadn't called back to complete the thought. I gave a laugh; knowing the two of them, they were most likely in the middle of a romantic interlude when they remembered to call. *Finish the message? Maybe later.* I can hear his voice saying the words.

I opened up the laptop and turned it on. Amazingly enough, I managed to connect to the Internet and find my e-mail. I smiled. Sam had sent me a letter. I opened it and read it.

As my first e-mail, it really wasn't anything special; he said nothing that I hadn't heard him say in person. Seeing his words in print, though, made them seem more real. It was a short letter; I knew he was having a difficult time at the hospital, so when I imagined him sitting down at his desk and taking the time from his hellish job to write, it made me feel wanted.

Hi, Sweetness. Glad you got there safely and glad Claude was able to show you how to use your birthday present. I'll bet you are surfing the Web right now. :) Keep in touch and remember to be careful. Love, Sam.

I put my hand up to the screen and ran my fingers over his words. Then I laughed at my folly and got dressed to meet Deirdre and Mitch.

It wasn't until I was walking out the door that I realized I should have sent him a reply. So I turned around and sat back at the desk. It took me longer than I would have thought to send the resulting message.

Mon Cher, I enjoyed your e-mail very much. They say a girl never forgets her first and you were mine. I am taking care and will be meeting Deirdre and Mitch in just a few minutes. I send you many many kisses and hugs. And I miss you. Yours, Viv

"Sorry to be late, Deirdre," I said as I sat down at the booth in the bar. "I had to send an e-mail. Where's Mitch?"

She looked at me. "Getting us a drink, I think." She looked across the room and spotted him, her face softening into a smile. "Yes, there he is." Then she blinked. "Did you say you were sending an e-mail?"

"*Oui.* I was sending e-mail." I sounded smug

and was pleased at how easily the words came from my mouth.

"Is this a new development?"

I smiled. "Yes, Sam gave me a laptop for my birthday."

"So you liked the surprise?" Mitch set three glasses of wine on the table, leaned over, and gave me a kiss. Then he sat down next to her, draping his arm lightly over the back of the seat. She leaned into him slightly, making sure to maintain body contact. I sighed and wondered if my sister knew how lucky she was to have such a partner.

"He was telling us about it on the way to the airport last month and I have to admit we both wondered what you would do with it."

"I'd not have known if it were not for Claude." Then I put my hand to my mouth. "Oh, dear, I had forgotten about him. We will want him with us, I think, for whatever we will be doing."

Mitch got up again. "I'll ring his room."

Deirdre and I both sipped our wine while he was gone. "Oh, and I wanted to thank you for the lovely necklace you gave me. I love it."

She gave me a warm smile. "I thought you might."

"Wherever did you find it?"

"I had it made special for you, of course. It's not as good a present as Sam gave you, of course, nor near as useful. How is he?"

"Sam?" I felt my mouth curve into a smile. "He is fine, he was the one to whom I was sending the e-mail."

She gave me a curious look, and I sensed that she wanted to ask me about our relationship. I did not know what to say so I turned the tables on her. "I see that you and Mitch are together again. I am glad you were able to work it out. You have no idea how lucky you are in him."

"Oh, but I do." Her eyes glowed with affection. "He is everything I ever dreamed of, everything I have ever wanted. And he seems to feel the same. So it is possible, Vivienne, for our kind to hold together."

I wanted to ask her how she managed, but Mitch returned at that moment, took his spot next to her again, and the opportunity for girl talk was gone. Instead she gave a small laugh and jumped back to our earlier topic. "E-mail. I can't even imagine it. You must be a quick learner."

I laughed, the high-pitched peals filling the room. "After I get over the initial culture shock, yes, I suppose I am. While you, on the other hand," and I reached across the table and touched Mitch's hand, "you do not seem to be able to leave a complete message."

They exchanged a look. "I told you," Deirdre said, "that you should have called back and left the end of the message."

"Yes, dear," Mitch said meekly and they both laughed as if at a private joke. I smiled weakly, feeling as I always did in their presence, totally superfluous.

"So," I said politely, waiting a second or two for them to finish with their laughter, "you spoke with Lily? Will she let us see Victor?"

Deirdre nodded, her voice growing tight. "Yes, I spoke with Lily. And it was not easy. She tried to keep us away as vehemently as I hear she did you. But fortunately Victor was in the room when I called and he recognized my voice. He wants to meet with us in about an hour at the Orchid." She sighed and leaned farther into Mitch, running a hand on his thigh, seeking comfort, I thought. "That girl has got a chip on her shoulder a mile wide. But Victor is her soft spot. It's good to know that there is at least one person to whom she doesn't delight in saying no."

I smiled. "I liked her. She has great spirit."

"More than anyone needs," Deirdre said and I stifled a laugh. *And it's good to know that there's someone in the world who doesn't think you're perfect, Sister.* "No one can have too much spirit, especially at times like these." That thought sobered me. "Now, before we meet with Victor would you like to tell me what happened in England?"

"Starting without me?" Claude loomed over us and I looked up and smiled.

"Not at all, *mon chou,* please," and I patted the leather seat next to me, "have a seat and join us."

He laughed. "Even if I were able to get into there, Vivienne, how on earth would you pry me out again? No, I'll need a . . . yeah, there's one." He looked around, spotted a suitable chair and grabbed it, turning it around so that he could straddle it while leaning his arms on the upper rail. "Much better."

Mitch nodded to Claude and began his story. "There's not much to tell, actually. We had been at the pub to close up. It'd been a long night and we were anxious to get home so we weren't paying all that much attention. He was waiting inside the door. We never had a clue that he was there. No scent, no sound. He jumped at Deirdre first and that was his mistake. I snapped his neck before he even reached her." He leaned over and kissed her on the tip of the nose. "To be honest it all happened so quickly that at first we didn't realize what his weapon of choice was and when we did it was disconcerting. We've kept a fairly low profile there, not taking our victims too close to home and maintaining as normal-seeming a life as possible. And we'd been gone for so long. The implication that he knew we had moved back is frightening. I'd have preferred he'd been a common thief; at least that sort of crime is understandable. But this—" He looked around to see if anyone was nearby, but with the exception of us, the bar was deserted. Regardless, he lowered his voice. "This was a deliberate and concerted effort to kill vampires specifically. I don't like it."

"What did you do with the body?" Claude spoke up from his backward perch.

"Dumped it in an alley in the rough part of town and made it look like someone had attempted to rob him. He had no identification on him at all. No passport, no driver's license, nothing to give me any hint at all why he wanted to kill us. He didn't speak, so I can't even tell you if he was local or imported."

"And then we heard your news, Vivienne. And Lily's." Mitch shook his head and took a drink of his Scotch. "All of these are very much carefully timed and engineered events. To hear that it all may be a plan executed by some sort of international terrorist group doesn't come as a surprise to me."

"But why?" I asked the question, knowing of course that he would not have an answer. "Why kill us? And why now? It makes no sense, Mitch. We have, most of us, been around for centuries and despite all the books and movies about hunting us, very little of that has ever gone on. We lead our lives side by side with the humans and they never know we are there."

Deirdre nodded. "That's true. I have been wondering the same thing myself. Why us? And why now?"

Claude shrugged. "Don't ask me, I'm the new kid on the block. Mitch? Any thoughts?"

"I don't know, Claude. There must be a reason, there always is. But I'll be damned if I can figure it out. And"—he looked at his watch—"we had better get a cab or we'll be late to meet Victor."

Thirty-four

Victor met us at the front door of the Blackened Orchid. He looked like his old self; his eyes were clear and he stood erect and confident. In fact, he was so very much changed from the last time I had seen him that I stared at him a little too long.

"What's the matter, Vivienne?" he said, laughing at me and gesturing all of us into the bar. "You look as if you've seen a ghost."

"Not a ghost, Victor," I said, kissing him lightly on both cheeks. "Just someone who hasn't been around for a while. And I for one am glad to have you back." I looked over to Lily where she stood, arms folded, behind the bar. "If this is your doing, Lily, I thank you."

She shrugged. "He woke up like this. Stubborn old man," and she gave him a tender smile to soften the words, "he wouldn't listen to me when I said that seeing all of you might not be a great idea."

"But of course it's a great idea, girl." Victor brushed at his black suede jacket. "It's a party of sorts. And Vivienne just loves a good party. Don't you, my dear?"

I smiled, not quite sure where he was going with this. But I had no doubt that this was the old Victor, the one who was capable of making me faint at our first meeting, simply by looking at me.

"And for our party we have a wonderful guest list. Deirdre and Mitch, two of our finest rogues." He nodded in their direction and Mitch scowled at him. "Pour Mitch a Scotch on the rocks, Lily, my dear, and give your mother and Vivienne a glass of that nice red wine we bought the other day. As for Claude." Victor clapped a hand on Claude's shoulder. "My former jailer, words cannot express how pleased I am to see you again. And in such fine mettle." He looked Claude up and down, then turned again to Lily. "I believe Claude's poison of choice is port. And while you're at it, please pour one for me."

He watched us all as we went to the bar to claim our drinks. "What is this all about?" I whispered to Lily but she just shrugged.

"I have no idea, Vivienne." She did not bother to lower her voice. "This is what I warned you about. He's worse today, but I couldn't keep you from coming. He was determined to see you all."

I nodded. "Victor," I said, sipping my wine, "can you tell us anything about the Others?"

He laughed and his eyes shifted around. "But I just did, Vivienne. There's Deirdre and Mitch and . . ." He stopped and shook his head, losing just a bit of his confidence, and my hopes for an easy solution plummeted. "But that's not what you wanted to know, is it? You wanted to know about the Others."

"Yes, Victor, that's it. Can you please tell us everything you know about the Others?" I made my voice as calm as possible; I saw now what Lily meant about him being difficult. Getting any information from Victor was going to be quite a task. I motioned to the others to move away and they did so, collecting in the far corner of the bar where Victor couldn't see them and be distracted.

"Think back," I urged. "It wasn't all that long ago, only a little over two hundred years. Do you remember Paris? The revolution? Max's journals mention a group called the Others that existed at that time."

"Yes." A wide smile crossed his face and his eyes focused again. "Max was always scratching away in those ridiculous journals. 'It's not as if anyone is ever going to read these, Max,' I would say. And he would get angry with me. He was always angry with me. Much of the time he was angry with me about you, Vivienne. You were such a lovely young thing then. So sweet, so innocent—he struggled so to try to keep you that way. But you wouldn't let him."

I snorted. "I? Innocent? I hardly think so. You must be thinking of some other time, some other Vivienne, perhaps?"

"Oh, but you were. That silly swan's head you were wearing and the way you danced and sang, you were so full of joy and youth and laughter." He paused for a second. "Max came dressed as a monk and I was the grim reaper. And you were a dancing swan." He chuckled to himself. "What was his name?"

I had a difficult time following his reasoning. "Whose name?"

"That man you danced with at the party. You must remember him, Vivienne. He was a doctor,

I think. A handsome bastard in any event. And you, ah, you were particularly entranced with him, as I remember. And Max was furious."

"Eduard."

"And his last name was?"

"DeRouchard."

He snapped his fingers. "Yes. That was it exactly." His eyes glowed in triumph over such a simple memory and I sighed. Poor man, that he should be reduced to this state. And poor us, should we not be able to get the information we needed.

Then the glow faded. "And you remember that we talked about the Others, don't you, Vivienne?"

"No."

"Yes, you do."

"No." I paused a second.

Victor smiled encouragingly. "Go on. I know you remember this. It was important."

I bit my lip. "Wait, I do remember that you spoke of getting all the others together and forming an organization to safeguard our lives and goals. And I laughed at you. But that was just a phrase, wasn't it? The others had been drawn there, by all the blood and the death. Just like carrion crows, you said."

He gave me a keen look. "If I said the Others, that is what I meant. Do not blame me if you did not understand."

"And did you meet with the Others, Victor? While you were in Paris?"

"Yes, I did. The evening after that silly party of yours. Max and I and Eduard and the rest of the Others all sat down—"

"No, Victor. Eduard cannot have been there.

You must be getting it confused with the party. Eduard was at the party, that is true. And that is where you saw him. He wouldn't have been at your meeting."

"You were so young, Vivienne, so innocent. Max was angry that you were so trusting. He said he thought he'd taught you better, that after Diego, you would have learned your lesson." Victor's voice was trembling and Lily came over next to him. She picked up his hand and put it to her mouth, kissing the palm, and he smiled at her.

"Let's go sit down, okay?" she said. "And then we can talk some more. But at least we'll all be more comfortable that way."

Victor looked at me and smiled. "You see the way it is, Vivienne? She orders me around. I should spank her like the young impertinent girl she is."

"Later, darling." She stuck her tongue out at him and he gave a loud laugh.

Deirdre gave a small cough and I looked over at her. Even in the dimness of the bar lights I could see that she was blushing and I chuckled to myself. What an interesting evening this was turning out to be.

Lily settled us in at a small round table. She set another glass of port in front of him and caught my eye. "Keep going." She mouthed the words to me over his head. "He's fine."

"I have to apologize, Victor. I do not remember what happened at this meeting. And I do not remember that Eduard was there."

"Of course you don't remember. You weren't at the meeting. But Eduard was. Of this I am quite sure. He had to be. He is the leader of the Others."

"Eduard? How could he have been? He was human."

Victor laughed. "You were so young, Vivienne, and so innocent. He is not a human. He is not a vampire, either. But a combination of both, a crossbreed, if you will. The Others are just exactly what their name implies, something other than what previously existed.

"Somehow they had learned how to prolong human life, but without having any of the bad aspects of the vampire, primarily that of the detrimental effects of sunlight. And they could go for much longer periods of time before they needed to feed.

"Unfortunately, the process only kept the mind alive indefinitely. Eventually the body would begin to deteriorate and they would need to transfer their life force into a human baby, preferably one fathered by themselves. The baby would then grow at an accelerated rate and within ten years become that same being." He shook his head. "I do not profess to understand how this was done; all I'd ever managed to learn was that the process was possible. They refused to share their knowledge."

"But Eduard can't have been one of them. His body showed no signs of deterioration."

"It would not necessarily show at first. But I remember that they all bore a scar."

My heart stopped. "A scar?"

"Yes, across their throat. From the transfer, you see. Eduard bears that scar even today, I'm sure. And I'm surprised that you never noticed it."

"But you speak of him as if he were still alive. He is dead, Victor, I saw his body. Executed."

"Yes, that was Max's idea, I fear. It seemed a simple solution at the time, eliminate the rival organization's leader and the rest would succumb. And Max hated him for the influence he had over you. But, we hadn't known at the time, that one of Eduard's breeders had given birth recently. Nor that she was skilled enough to effect the transfer with one who had been dead for some time. But she did and she was and in just a short time he was back. The breeder stayed with him, I believe. You knew her. What was her name?"

I sat for a while and stared at Victor. How could he have known all of this for as long as he did and not tell me? But I knew that at least some of what he was telling me was true. It explained so much I had never understood.

"Monique?" I had not meant to say her name. I did not want to know.

"Yes, that was the breeder's name."

"But she was with *me*, she was my friend. She loved me."

Victor laughed. "You were so young and so innocent, Vivienne."

I sighed. I was getting very weary of hearing that phrase.

"Don't you see?" Victor continued. "She gave you exactly what Eduard wanted her to, no less and no more. She was his creature from the first. And to the last. Everything that you did at that time and everything that you felt for both of them had been forced upon you by Eduard. Testing, I believe, whether his powers over us were developed enough to take control."

I closed my eyes and bit my lip. It was as if someone had torn down my life and left it in rubble on the ground. Everything that I thought I knew was wrong.

I thought Eduard had loved me and he had not. I thought Eduard had died, but he still lived. With the sole purpose of exterminating my kind. And Monique? I did not even want to think of the enormity of her betrayals.

"Oh, Victor," I whispered across the table to him, "why didn't you tell me? Don't you think I should have known?"

"There was no need for anyone to know. Max and I both feared that the Cadre would panic and overreact. I had control of the situation. And Monique seemed to have weaned herself away from Eduard's influence, so she was no danger to you or to us."

And what of Monique? When she had come back, it was at his command. She had stood by my side for the past ten years, watching, learning, and reporting, no doubt, on all of the Cadre's activities. And she had done it all for him.

Suddenly Angelo's words from last night came back to me.

"*. . . She love you if he let her, but don' you know, he won'. There be no love in this man. No love for you, no love for her, no love for that dead baby. A cold man. He not like me, Miss Vivienne. And no, not even like you. He somethin' diff'rent, somethin' new. Somethin'* other *than what he should be. . . .*"

"He knew all of this. How could he know?" My voice sounded small and frightened in the darkness.

"Who?"

"I met this man in a bar last evening—he called himself a bokor. He told me my future and he knew everything you just told me now. How is that possible?"

Lily and Victor exchanged glances. "Tell me," she said, her arms folded, "he wasn't named Angelo, was he?"

"Yes. Do you know him?"

"I swear, I'm going to wring his scrawny little neck. Rest easy, Vivienne," Lily said with a dry smile, "his story at least is nothing out of the ordinary. There's nothing supernatural about it; unless you consider eavesdropping a mystical talent."

Suddenly the tension in the room eased and we all laughed softly.

I did not mind that the joke was on me. "He seemed so sincere, so knowledgeable."

Victor opened his mouth.

"Don't, Victor." I shot him a warning look. "I am neither young nor innocent. And I really do not want to hear you say it again."

Mitch walked over to us, followed by Deirdre and Claude.

"Forget Angelo," he said to me, "forget the past and the future. Forget about youth and innocence. Or the lack thereof. What we need to know is how to get rid of this Eduard once and for all. Right now. Just exactly how powerful is he, Victor? Say on a scale of one to ten, with ten being the strongest?"

"Getting right to the heart of the matter, Mitch?" Victor smiled at him. "You were always very good at that." He thought for a while. "On a good day, he is probably a nine. It's hard to gauge, of course. And I can only base it on my own peak strength."

"And how would he compare to all of us?"

"If you were older, Mitch, and more experienced, I'd say that you would stand a chance. Claude is an unknown. Deirdre might be capable of defeating him with a little luck. Lily too." He looked over at me. "I fear, Vivienne, that you would be helpless before him. He has already demonstrated quite aptly that he can manipulate you."

I looked away from him, knowing that what he said was true. I could no more strike against Eduard or even Monique than I could against myself.

"What about you, Victor?" I said. "How do you rate?"

He shrugged. "I was always stronger than Eduard. And so was Max. But Max is dead. And I am not all here." He gave a bitter, humorless laugh. "As I know you have all so aptly observed at one time or another. Eduard, on the other hand, is unimpaired by any disability and has been waiting for hundreds of years for this opportunity. He hates us. And will not rest until we are all dead."

"So there's no hope of defeating him?" Deirdre sounded indignant. "I cannot believe that, Victor. There must be a way. There is always a way. Why did it take him so long to strike at us?"

"I held him off." Victor pounded his fist against his thigh. "Max and I, between the two of us, kept him at bay. But Max is dead. And I . . ." His voice trailed off, his face twisted up, and he put his head down on the table and began to cry.

Lily sighed. "Thanks, Mom," she said. She urged Victor up from his chair and wrapped an arm around his waist. "I'm going to take him home now. I was afraid this was going to happen. Still, you all have what you wanted from him and you can leave us in peace again so that I can patch him up. Until next time." She nodded to Claude. "Lock up the front door when you leave, please. The keys are hanging on a ring inside the kitchen door."

I reached out and touched her arm. "Lily, take care of him."

"Yes, by all means, Lily, take care of him. Or I will."

I turned. Eduard stood in the open door.

Thirty-five

He was as beautiful as ever. Even now that I knew him for the evil he truly was, it made no difference. Victor had been right, I was helpless before him. And what made it worse was that he knew it.

"Vivienne." He crossed the room with his typical grace, picked up my hand, and kissed it. "You have not changed a bit, my dear."

I wrenched my hand away from his grasp, lifted it up to his face, and attempted to slap him. The blow glanced off him as if he were made of air.

Eduard laughed. "Yes, you have not changed. You are as young and pretty as that night we first met. And, I fear, as stupid. You are such a simpleton; I never cease to be amazed that you manage to survive. Tell me, Vivienne, have you ever had an original thought in your life? Beyond your petty vanities and games, that is? Did you not bother to listen to what Victor told you? You can't touch me now, none of you can."

He turned to where the rest of them stood staring. "Just the same," and he motioned with his head, "I'd feel better if you all would kindly step over here, in front of the bar, where I can keep an eye on you."

Deirdre clenched her fists and Mitch snarled, but they both moved as he ordered, followed by Claude and Lily, still supporting the weeping Victor. "Such a lovely family grouping," he said. "You must be proud, Victor, of your children. Or rather Max's children and your grandchildren. That is how you vampires trace your lineage, isn't it?"

"But no, Victor is not himself today, is he? Poor Victor, he's lost so much over the years. And virtually none of it was my doing. But I rejoiced in it all the same."

Eduard walked over to Deirdre and took her chin into his hand. "You, my dear, did me the kindest favor in killing Max. I think I'll let you die quickly as a reward."

"Why are you doing this, Eduard?" I forced the words out of my mouth. His control over me was frightening, mind numbing in its intensity. And from the expressions on the other faces, I knew that they felt the same.

He ran his hand down Deirdre's face, then caressed her neck and breast, watching the expression in Mitch's eyes change from anger to uncontrollable rage to helplessness. "Because," he pulled his hand away from her and laughed, "I can. None of you can lift a finger to stop me. And because worthless creatures who possess powers they refuse to use deserve to die."

He shook his head. "That's not exactly it, of course. When I rid the world of vampires, I will be a hero. I have always wanted to be a hero. Yes, maybe it's just as simple as that. Just think how grateful the human race will be. I will have freed them from their main predator." He bared his teeth in a humorless smile. "When the vampires are gone, then my kind will be the superior species without question. And we have no qualms about using our powers."

He looked around at all of us. "Is no one going to say, 'You are crazy, Eduard'? Or 'You'll never get away with this'? I must confess that I'm disappointed."

"I will say it."

All eyes turned to a dark figure in the doorway. As it limped haltingly into the room, I recognized the ravaged and burnt body. "Monique!" Despite all that Victor had said about her, despite the fact that I knew the truth of her, I felt a rush of joy that she still lived.

She advanced on Eduard, clutching a large knife in her charred hand. "I worked for you, Eduard, for all those centuries. I lied for you, bore you the body you bear even now. I killed for you and," her eyes darted over to me, "betrayed ones that I love. But I will serve you no more."

Eduard laughed. "Not dead yet, Monique? I'd have thought that either the explosion or the sun would have finished you. Have you looked into a mirror lately, my dear? Such a disgusting sight. You have grown repulsive and now that your duplicity is revealed, you are useless as well."

She gave a low growl and raised the knife. "I gave you the life you now have, Eduard, I can take it away."

His face twisted into a half smile. "I don't think so, Monique. What you can do, though, is turn that knife on yourself. Just drive it into your heart and it will all be over."

Her hand trembled and she licked her lips nervously.

"Now, Monique," Eduard commanded, "do it now. Turn the knife around," his voice sounded almost tender, and he nodded to encourage her. "Yes, that's right."

Her wrist twisted around and the blade of the knife was pointed at her heart. "No," she whimpered. "I do not want to die, not like this."

Her eyes caught mine, pleading.

"Do not do it, Monique, fight him," I whispered, but already the tip of the knife was entering her chest.

"I'm sorry, Vivienne," she said, "so very sorry."

"Enough of this foolishness." Eduard spun around and drove the knife into her heart. She looked down in disbelief as her blood spouted from the wound. Then she gave a single gasp and fell to the floor at his feet.

He kicked her body out of the way and it slid across the room, leaving a trail of blackened skin and red blood.

I held back a sob. *Poor little lamb,* I thought, *I am sorry too.*

Eduard wiped his bloody hands on the nearest tablecloth. "There," he said nodding, "That is better. She really was too ugly to live. But," he turned to face Lily now, "you ladies are quite lovely. And now that Monique is dead, I will need companionship. Should I take one of you or all three?"

Something inside me snapped. Eduard was going to kill us all, as he had Monique. Right here and soon. He had aptly demonstrated his powers and there was no way any of us would survive this encounter. One glance at the faces of the others confirmed this. We were all helpless before him and we would all die.

With that thought my fear of him faded away. If he was going to kill us all, then fear did not help. And if I was going to lose my life, I would at least lose it with as much style and panache as I lived it.

"Je t'emmerde, espece de porc a la manque!" The words came out through clenched teeth, but he heard them and spun around to face me with a snarl.

"You are a stupid cow, Vivienne. You can't hope to gain anything with trivial insults."

"No," I said, "I do not want to gain anything. And all I can see is that what you are doing is stupid, Eduard. Just kill us and be done with it." I rolled my eyes and shrugged. "None of us really wish to stand around and have you taunt us for hours before we die. It is trite and boring and I'd have expected better from you."

Lily looked at me and snickered. "Good one, Vivienne."

I saw a flash of anger and doubt enter his eyes; his thoughts were easy to read. I should not have been able to defy him. I smiled and Lily laughed again. He backhanded her without a second glance and she crumpled to the floor.

Victor's head snapped up. There were no tears in his eyes now, just anger and hatred. And I felt a surge of hope. *Yes, Victor,* I urged him silently, *get angry.*

Eduard did not notice that Victor had revived. His first mistake.

I pushed against his control, testing the limits. He seemed just a bit weaker now, perhaps the use of his power against Monique had tired him. Under the surface of his steely control, I felt the undercurrent of his anger. If I pushed him hard enough, if I goaded him into attacking me, he just might drop his guard.

I caught Mitch's eye and he gave a nod. He understood what I was attempting—it was a comfort to know that I wasn't risking my life on idle chance.

Yes, it was a simple ploy, but then I was, by his words, a simpleton. Stupid and trivial.

I smiled again, a broad grin that exposed my fangs. And step by step I inched up on him, still smiling.

"You can't frighten me, Vivienne. I know you too well for that."

"You know nothing, Eduard. And you are nothing. You feel superior because you can live forever?" I snapped my fingers and he jumped. "There is nothing difficult about living forever. Even someone as stupid as I can manage that. And I can do it without stooping to murdering my own babies, or the woman who birthed them."

I kept moving in on him, each step becoming more difficult than the last.

He was surrounded now by a dimly glowing cloud, his power concentrating and forming a shield around him. But I continued to force my way to him, gratified to see the shield waver and weaken in spots. He was not totally invincible.

Mitch gave a sharp intake of breath. Had he seen the shield? Did he see the weakened areas?

No matter. I could not worry about any of them. It was taking all my energy and all my will to continue to push against him.

I smiled, holding my eyes on Eduard's, advancing step by painful step into the shining sphere of his power. I barely noticed or cared that small rivulets of blood were now trailing down from my eyes and my mouth.

"Tell me, Eduard, *mon chou,* does the murder of innocents make you important? Does it make you smart? Does it make you a hero?"

I pushed. I moved forward. I smiled.

And Eduard was beginning to sweat. I could see the beads form on his forehead and his upper lip.

"You can't do this, Vivienne, you don't have the strength to fight me. I have held you in my arms and I have made you love me. You can't act against me."

There was the key. We were, despite the years between us, bound together. I kept smiling. "You are right, Eduard. I cannot act against you, I love you." I held my arms out to him, pitching my voice at its lowest and most persuasive. He had forgotten something quite important: the ties of blood and passion that bound me to him held him also. His second mistake.

He took an awkward step forward.

"Kiss me, Eduard," I whispered to him. "Kiss me like you used to on those long lovely nights we spent together." I moaned, breathing my words on his skin. "You remember them, Eduard, I know you do. You remember them as well as I do, I know you do. And you want them to return as much as I. Don't you?"

He gave a small nod, barely visible.

"Then kiss me, Eduard. Nothing else matters."

He stepped into my outstretched arms and I clasped him to me in an iron grip. "Kiss me." It was a command this time; one he could not disobey.

And then Eduard put his lips to mine. His third and final mistake.

Instantly, I opened my mouth and sank my fangs deep into his upper lip, then into his lower lip. He struggled to pull away, but the pain dragged him back to me. And I smiled as my mouth filled with his blood, as his eyes grew more pained and confused. *Now,* I thought, *I don't care which one of you takes him. But one of you must. Now!*

I pulled away from him just as Victor sprang up and knocked him to the floor.

I stood back to give them room, picking the small bits of Eduard's flesh from my canines.

Victor and Eduard fought, neither of them able to fully overcome the other and neither of them able to let go. Eduard's glowing shield shot to life again and encompassed them both, locking them together in a deadly embrace.

"Do something," Lily whispered. "He can't keep this up."

Mitch moved toward the struggling figures and was thrown back. "I can't, Lily. I'm sorry."

"If you can't, I will."

"No!" Victor's voice was heavy and deep. "Stay away!"

And as we watched, Victor began to dissolve

into a mist. It curled around inside Eduard's shield and began to match its glow.

The expression on Eduard's face was triumphant at first. Then as he saw the mist curling around him, the smile on his face changed from the grin of victory to the wince of fear.

"Look," I whispered, "what is that? And which one of them is doing it?"

At first I thought it was a trick of the light, but no, there it was again. A tiny lick of flame, followed by another and another.

Soon, the mist that had been Victor became flames and then an inferno, burning violently within the walls Eduard had built around himself for protection. By the time he realized what was happening, his skin had scorched and blackened beyond repair. He turned to me, his eyes pleading, his lips moving, begging me to save him.

I smiled. And shook my head. "This, my dear Eduard, is for what you did to Monique. And to me."

By now the flesh seemed to be melting from his bones. A death's head turned to me again as if in disbelief.

Then Eduard gave one great agonized scream and lay still. The shield fluttered and faded out.

The flames that had been Victor flared up around the lifeless body of Eduard, looming over him in triumph. Their roar was deafening. Then they subsided and dropped back down, radiating out from the corpse like water rings, spreading across the floor, thinner and thinner, until they dissolved.

Everything was totally silent until Lily choked

back a sob. "Victor," she whispered, "you stubborn old man. What will I do without you?"

Deirdre put an arm around her and the girl buried her head against her mother's chest, sobbing quietly. "Hush," Deirdre said, her hands softly stroking Lily's back, the two of them slowly rocking back and forth.

Then Deirdre's head snapped up and she seemed to be listening. "Hush," she said again but with different meaning. "Wait," she said with a half smile, "do not mourn him yet, Lily. Open your eyes and look."

She pointed to the far corner of the room, where the smoke from the fire seemed to hang heavy and still in the air. Then it thickened and curled, moving across the room until it engulfed the girl and spun her about in a wild dance. And suddenly, so quickly that my eyes could not register the change, it was Victor, scorched and singed beyond all belief, but alive.

Mitch approached him and hooked an arm around his shoulders, carefully trying to avoid contact with his ravaged skin. "Good trick, Victor. Now let's get you home."

I walked over and nudged Eduard's remains with the tip of my shoe. The body shook just a little and I jumped back. Then as I watched, it lost its resemblance to a human body and dissolved into a pile of ashes.

I knelt down next to it, gathered a little of the ash in my hand, and held it to my face. "All in all, Eduard, it would have been better if you had accepted the hero's death there on Place du Carroussel. But as I loved you once, may you rest in peace."

Epilogue

It is not really over, of course. The Others still exist and I suspect that Eduard's death will only slow them down for a short while. We will never be able to rest again until we can be sure that they will not retaliate.

But we have time now. Victor bought us that at great cost, and we must not waste it. We need to plan and to safeguard those of our kind still remaining. Mitch has moved back into the leadership of the Cadre, to develop it into something different than it had been. He has assigned each of us posts of duty, where we can watch for signs of the Others. Victor and Lily will remain in New Orleans, at least until his scorched body heals. Claude will go back to New York City. And Mitch and Deirdre will return once again to England. If a new Cadre headquarters is established, it will be based in England. At Whitby, by the sea. A site so obvious that no one would ever suspect.

And I have been assigned to Paris.

Now that Eduard is gone, and his influence over me has been burned away, I feel purified. I realize that my inability to love was nothing but a pretense on my part. A defense against being hurt. I am three hundred years old. And suspect that I have not yet lived.

I have begun to know that life is pain as well as joy. And that you cannot embrace one without letting a little of the other in as well.

And as for love, well, I do not know. Sometimes, as I lie in Sam's arms and I feel the warmth of him flow through me, I think it may be close. And I take comfort from the fact that if we are capable of changing into fire and back again, then we must also be capable of love.

Sam has come to Paris with me, for a time, at least. He and I walk, hand in hand, through the rain-drenched streets, visiting places of history. I tell him stories of the life I led, sometimes ending with laughter and sometimes with tears.

I find that the city has changed in many ways and in many more has remained the same. And life is good.

Exactly as it should be.

ENTER THE WORLD OF KAREN E. TAYLOR'S VAMPIRE LEGACY

BLOOD SECRETS (Book One)

Allow me to introduce myself. My name is Deirdre Griffin, and I'm a vampire. Currently I'm living in Manhattan, and I spend my evenings at the Ballroom of Romance, where I satisfy my blood lust with weekly feedings. Unlike other vampires, I *never* drain my victims. But it seems there's another vampire on the loose who *is* his draining his victims—and pointing the finger of suspicion at me! What's a woman to do? If you're a vampire like me, you use your feminine wiles to hunt him down. . . .

BITTER BLOOD (Book Two)

Remember me? Deirdre Griffin, *vampire?* After living in London for two years, I'm back in my favorite city. But life in New York's no picnic in the park. It seems that a group of vampires wants revenge against me for killing their leader. What's worse, they're using my ex-lover, Detective Mitch Greer, as bait, and the only way I can save him is by converting him into a vampire like me. . . .

BLOOD TIES (Book Three)

It's me again: Deirdre Griffin, *vampire.* When we last met, my lover, Mitch Greer, had finally become a vampire. Now we're back on the streets of New York, at the request of the Cadre, a secret society of ancient vampires, because another series of murders is taking place. It turns out this guy isn't just killing humans, he's also killing vampires. . . .

BLOOD OF MY BLOOD (Book Four)

I'm back. Deirdre Greer, *vampire*—formerly Deirdre Griffin. I've married Mitch, promising to love him for all eternity, but now he's vanished from our backwoods Maine cabin. As I embark on a search for my beloved, traveling to the French Quarter of New Orleans, I uncover a baffling trail—a trail supposedly left by me. Who is the shadowy, eerily familiar figure lurking in the fringes of my life? What does she want of me? And what has she done with Mitch?

THE VAMPIRE VIVIENNE (Book Five)

Allow me to introduce myself. My name is Vivienne Courbet, and I've been a vampire since 1719. Let me assure you, I don't look a day over twenty-nine. You're probably more familiar with my blood sister, Deirdre Griffin, but she's on holiday right now so I thought I'd take center stage and tell you my life story. Recently I was appointed figurehead of the Cadre, a vampire fellowship in Manhattan, and my duties haven't demanded much—until now. You see, war has been declared against the Cadre, and a close friend of mine was among the first fatalities. I must put an end to this rebellion before I lose anyone else. My handsome human lover, Dr. John Samuels, will assist me in my efforts—and anything else I should need. As of yet, I'm unsure if our enemies are human or vampire. But when I find out, I vow that blood will be spilled. . . .

ACKNOWLEDGMENTS

Big thanks as always are due to my husband, Pete, and my sons, Brian and Geoff, for being willing to forego home-cooked meals and clean laundry during the writing process. Thank you also to Mary and Dave for their help with the French phrases; to John for his last-minute tidbits of advice; to John Scognamiglio, my wonderful editor; to Cherry Weiner, my fabulous agent; to Laura, just because; and to all the folks on sff.net who listened during IRC sessions, most especially Lena, who put up with more of my private wailing than anyone else. Take a bow, folks. Viv wouldn't have existed without your help and support.

ABOUT THE AUTHOR

Karen E. Taylor lives in Maryland with her husband, two sons, two cats, a dog, and a guinea pig. She is currently at work on the sixth book of The Vampire Legacy series (which will be a return to the narration of Deirdre Griffin-Greer) to be published by Pinnacle Books in September 2002

Karen loves to hear from her readers. You may contact her c/o Pinnacle Books. Please enclose a self-adressed, stamped envelope if you wish to receive a response. You may also visit the official Vampire Legacy Web site at http://www.karenetaylor.com and e-mail her from there.